The Final Service

He arrived unannounced,
where and when she needed him most...

Gary W. Moore

Especially for Bev!

Savas Beatie
California

Copyright © 2016 by Gary W. Moore

All rights reserved. No part of this publication may be reproduced, stored in a retrieval system, or transmitted, in any form or by any means, electronic, mechanical, photocopying, recording, or otherwise, without the prior written permission of the publisher.

Library of Congress Cataloging-in-Publication Data

Names: Moore, Gary W. (Gary Warren), 1954- author.
Title: The final service / by Gary W. Moore.
Description: First edition. | El Dorado Hills, California: Savas Beatie LLC, [2016]
Identifiers: LCCN 2016001854| ISBN 9781611212945 (hardcover: alk. paper) | ISBN 9781611212952 (ebk.)
Subjects: LCSH: Middle-aged women—-Fiction. | Grief—Fiction. | Self-realization in women—Fiction. | Self-actualization (Psychology) in women—Fiction.
Classification: LCC PS3613.O5574 F56 2016 | DDC 813/.6—dc23
LC record available at http://lccn.loc.gov/2016001854

SB
Savas Beatie LLC
989 Governor Drive, Suite 102
El Dorado Hills, CA 95762
Phone: 916-941-6896 / (E-mail) sales@savasbeatie.com

05 04 03 02 01 5 4 3 2 1
First edition, first printing

FSC
www.fsc.org
MIX
Paper from responsible sources
FSC® C011935

Savas Beatie titles are available at special discounts for bulk purchases. For more details, contact us at Special Sales, 989 Governor Drive, El Dorado Hills, CA 95762, or please e-mail us at sales@savasbeatie.com, or visit our website at www.savasbeatie.com for additional information.

Advance Praise for *The Final Service*

"Gary W. Moore has a knack for telling our stories. Whether it's a dream interrupted in *Playing with the Enemy* or a personal journey of discovery in *Hey Buddy*, Moore tells us about ourselves while writing about others. Never is that more true than in *The Final Service*, where a father's misunderstood love nearly tears his daughter apart. Love doesn't always come in the shape we expect. If we're lucky, we realize that before it's too late."

— Steve Bertrand, WGN Radio, host of Steve Bertrand on Books

"A poignant story of redemption, the power of forgiveness, and the wisdom that comes later in life when we see our parents as they really are."

— Regine Schlesinger, WBBM Radio, Chicago

"*The Final Service* is a song of pain and grief and life and death. Author Gary W. Moore highlights the impact of war not only on the combatants themselves but on their families. Decades of sorrow, loss, and guilt erode human connections, but loyalty, understanding, and memory are the magical ties that reach beyond the grave. The parable of Sandy and her father Tom celebrates the complexities of love. Bravo to Gary for touching my crusty old heart."

— Joyce Faulkner, the award-winning author of *In the Shadow of Suribachi* and *Windshift*, and former President of Military Writers of America

"A compelling and endearing story about what matters most in a time when it matters most of all."

— James Riordan, author of *Break on Through: The Life and Death of Jim Morrison*

"*The Final Service* is an engaging read! As the son of a disabled World War Two vet, I readily related to some of Shadow's issues. My dad was my first hero, despite the limitations that came with a wooden leg, and like Shadow, my dad was also taken way too soon. I was glad she found the answers she'd been unknowingly seeking."

— Steve Rondinaro, former TV news anchor and longtime on-air host of Drum Corps International World Championship

"*The Final Service*, with love, compassion, and forgiveness at its core, is a poignant and emotionally powerful story that will touch your heart and your soul."

— Pamela Powell, Film Critic, www.reelhonestreviews.com

"How do you evaluate your parents? When we are children, we know nothing (or not enough to deal with it rationally) of the adult world. Whatever slights come our way can be magnified ten-fold. Do we remember the 100 trips to Little League games, or the one game when dad failed to show? Gary W. Moore's *The Final Service* also pays homage to our veterans, post-traumatic stress disorder, and our understanding of how to treat it. I read *The Final Service* in a single evening and did not want it to end. It is thoroughly satisfying with a wonderful message everyone should read and understand."

— Phil Angelo, *Kankakee Daily Journal*

"In *The Final Service*, Gary W. Moore reminds us why he's methodically laying claim to the designation of 'America's Storyteller.' Life, in Moore's various works, is never easy, but it's the journey that makes life worthwhile. He celebrates our foibles and our indiscretions through his characters by turning the mirror on ourselves so we better realize our own traits as we witness them in others. *The Final Service* is about all of us. We just don't realize that until we finish the last page."

— Michael Boo, Staff Writer, *Drum Corps International*

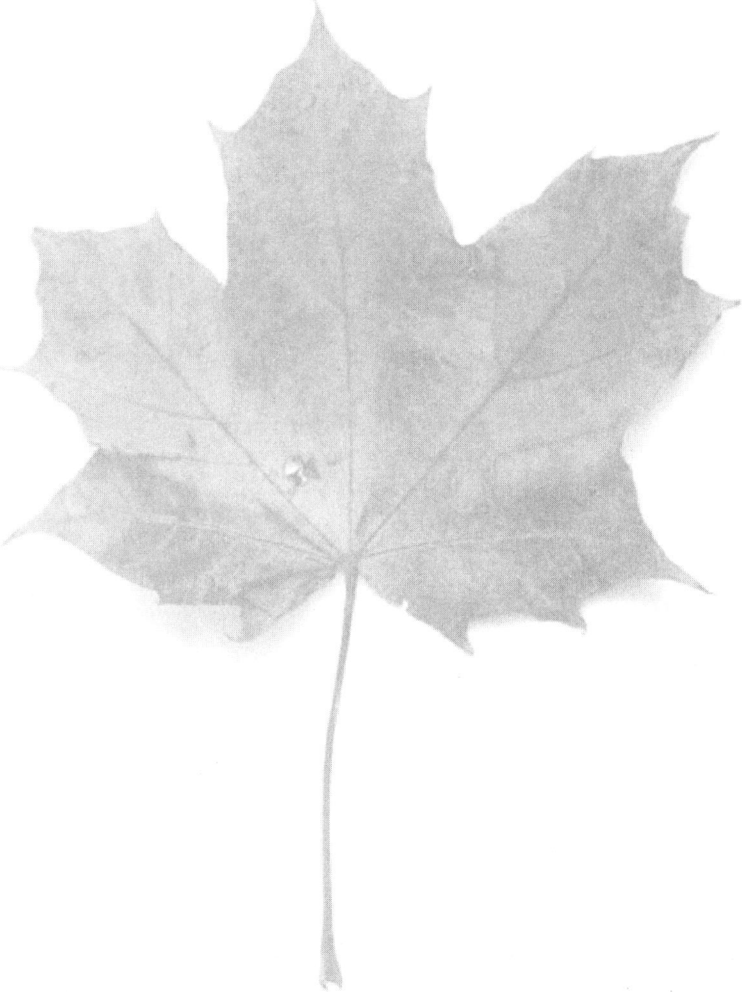

Author Gary W. Moore

Follow Gary on Social Media!

On Twitter @GaryWMoore721
Like *The Final Service* on Facebook
Like Gary W. Moore Author/Speaker on Facebook
Like *Playing with the Enemy* on Facebook
Like *Hey Buddy* on Facebook

Visit Gary at . . .

www.thefinalservice.com
www.playingwiththeenemy.com
www.garywmoore.com

Also visit Gary at …

www.cinemafundcapital.com
www.positivitypictures.com

Gary is available for books signings and discussions, as well as motivational and inspirational speaking engagements

Contact Gary at gary@garywmoore.com
or his publisher at sales@savasbeatie.com

For Caleb and Noah

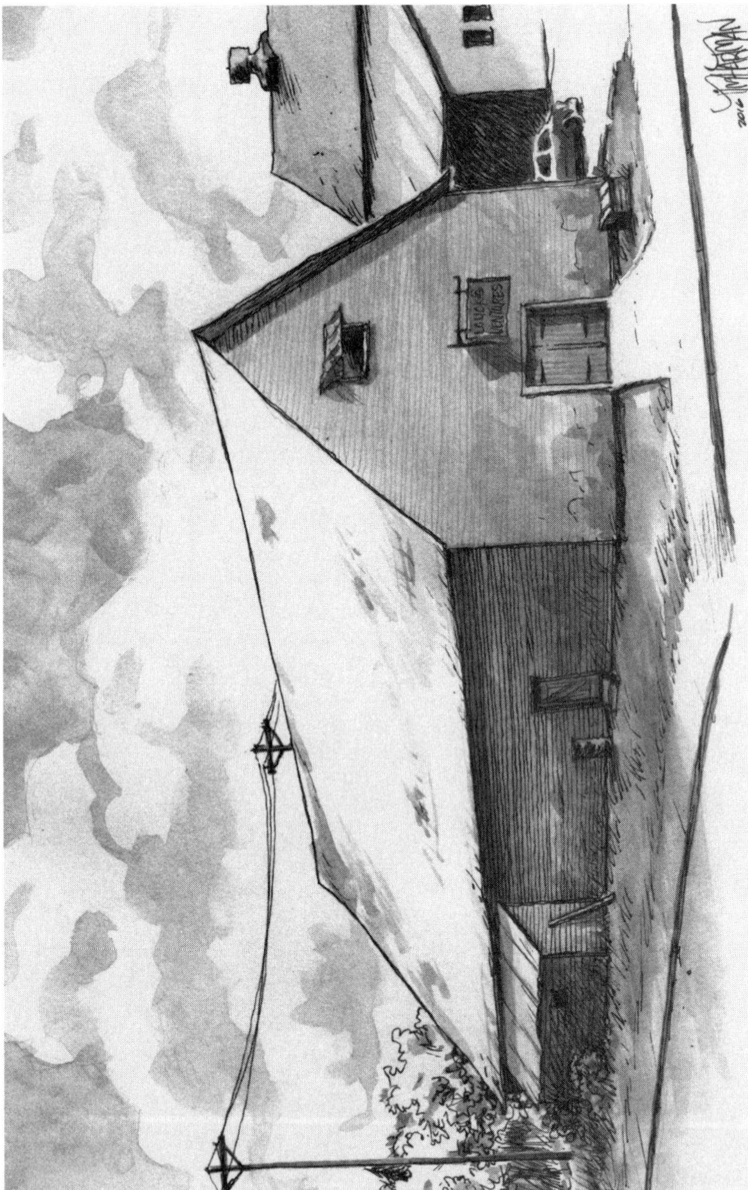

Contents

Prologue: June 6, 1944

ix

The Final Service

1

Afterword

169

Acknowledgments

172

Splooie!

and for Sandy

Go Big Red!

Prologue

June 6, 1944

"I'm not dying here and neither are you!"

The tall and lanky GI with closely cropped coal black hair turned his head to fix his amber eyes on his buddy standing to his right. "Got it?" he continued. He finished readjusting the chin strap of his helmet and put it back on his head. "Cover me. I'll cover you. We get off that beach fast. We'll make it through this day. That's the way it's going to be."

"Get ready! Three minutes!" boomed a voice behind them.

"There's no glory in this, Duke," replied Agno. "Only killing and dying. . ."

Agno's gentle reply almost passed unheard, suffocated mid-sentence by a cold salty wave of green seawater that broke over the bow of their landing craft to soak its occupants. The bow had dipped once more into yet another undulating foamy green valley of water before plowing its way up again as it headed toward a beach none of its occupants could see.

A man of few words, Duke shook the spray from his face without reply. What most men might blurt out in response, he simply kept to himself.

"... I've always hated boats," finished Agno as he wiped the spray away from his eyes.

By this time, so did most of the other nearly three-dozen seasick men in the Higgins Boat. The landing craft was only thirty-six feet long by eleven feet wide, powered by a 225-horsepower diesel engine that barely made ten knots under ideal circumstances. The choppy English Channel that early morning played on the vessel's tendency to sway and saw side to side. Most of the GIs were puking in their helmets or on the deck within minutes of climbing off the cargo net draped down the side of their troop transport ship. Because it had a flat bottom, the craft could run onto a flat shoreline. Once there, the steel ramp that doubled as a door at the bow would open to disgorge its human cargo to its fate. The invasion of Fortress Europe was underway.

"One minute!"

Duke gripped his M-1 Garand rifle and stared straight ahead. Soon enough, the hull would crunch across the shallow bottom, the ramp would drop with a hard thud into the sand, and they would have to scramble off that boat as fast as possible directly toward a determined enemy dug in on the bluffs just beyond. His jaw tightened at the thought. Another wave, this one bigger than the last, soaked the suffering men. The smell and taste of salt water filled Duke's nostrils. He wiped the corners of his eyes with his fingertips, spread his feet a bit farther apart for better balance, and waited.

Agno, an equally tall and strikingly handsome twenty-seven year-old Italian from New York, elbowed Duke's side. A sickly half-smile spread across Agno's face. "We're not dying here, huh? In other words, you want me to save your butt. Again."

"Thirty seconds! Get ready, men! When that door goes down Hell is going to break loose. Move inland. Do not stop!"

The landing craft had to hit the beach hard and fast, so none of the dozens of boats closing in on the shore slowed down during the final seconds of approach.

"Sure, you can save my butt again," replied Duke. "But you heard the lieutenant. When this door drops, we're going to catch Hell! Just keep moving and stay with me. We are going to kill a lot of Krauts today."

"Here we go!" yelled the man standing in front of Agno when the bottom of their landing craft began dragging across the gravelly Normandy bottom. Every man in the boat performed his own final ritual. Some said a Hail Mary, and others crossed themselves. A few prayed aloud, asking for salvation. The rest remained defiantly silent, absorbed in their thoughts. Metallic pings filled their ears as enemy bullets found the front of the boat.

A loud whistle blew when the boat finally ground to a halt and the steel door ten feet in front of Duke and Agno cranked open and dropped away, turning itself from a protective barrier into a ramp within seconds. As if as one, all three-dozen men moved simultaneously, the men in front spilling down the ramp into chest-deep water with the others pressing closely behind.

Duke and Agno were about to hit the ramp together when one of the men in front stumbled, cried out something indistinguishable, and fell in a bloody heap. Within a split second two other soldiers who had just left the ramp and were wading toward the sand staggered and slipped beneath it. The water churning around them turned from the gray reflective color of the overcast sky to a sickly pink.

Duke instinctively grabbed his friend by the arm and shoved him in the opposite direction, off the ramp to the right and into a chin-deep sea.

Bullets whizzed past their exposed heads and smacked into the plywood sides of the landing craft. A shorter soldier who had followed them off the right side of the ramp was unable to keep his head above water. Duke looked on helplessly as the man waved his hands wildly in the air before finally withdrawing them out of sight. It was as if they were all trapped in a slow motion nightmare, but instead of trying to escape the danger, Duke and his friend were moving into the lethal hail. The weight of their equipment and the depth of the water made for a miserably slow move onto the beach.

Once they managed to wade the last few yards to shore, Duke and Agno staggered a handful of yards before falling to the sand behind several freshly killed men. With one hand holding his helmet in place, Duke slowly lifted his head and peered up and down the beach. Chaos reigned in every direction. Scores of soldiers were frantically funneling themselves out of their own landing crafts to push through the water toward nonexistent cover. The giant bomb craters the navy had promised to scoop out of the flat beach were no where in sight. Instead the scenic landscape was carpeted with the dead and the dying, all of whom composed the first wave to hit the beach. Something was going terribly wrong.

The roar of the pounding surf combined with the throbbing engines and his own nerves to mute the gunfire crisscrossing Omaha Beach from more directions than Duke could count. Willing himself to look ahead, Duke focused his eyes on the bluffs about 100 yards distant. Twinkles of light representing machine gun and rifle fire blinked without respite, kicking up globs of sand from the beach and hunks of flesh from the men. Slowly, with each ticking second, the cacophony of fire increased until the thousands of individual rounds combined into one long, thunderous roar.

When he and Agno finally made it to the shoreline, their pace quickened. They focused on the rocks that separated the beach from the rocky incline, but their legs couldn't move as fast as their fear required.

"We can't stay here!" yelled Duke, who used his hand to point the direction. "Head to the right, Agno, toward the rocks!"

Agno nodded his understanding. Both men staggered to their feet and, hunched over as if moving into a stiff wind, set out for a rocky incline that offered at least some protection from the sheets of metal cutting the air all around them. They were halfway there when Agno stopped and straightened. Duke was preparing to shove his friend forward when he spotted a crimson stain spreading across the upper part of the back of his uniform.

Agno turned his head to meet Duke's stare. A surprised look crossed the dying man's face. "I'm hit," he murmured.

Duke dropped his M-1 and caught his friend as Agno's knees buckled. Cradling him under the arm pits, Duke dragged Agno the final few steps to the gravelly incline. With his back to the enemy, Duke pulled Agno's head onto his lap and tilted his friend's helmet back to look into his eyes. The entire front of Agno's uniform was bloody, and a red bubbly froth oozed from his pale lips.

"Don't leave me. Look at me, buddy! Say something! Stay awake! Stay awake!" screamed Duke. His heart begged Agno to speak, but his mind knew his frien was already gone.

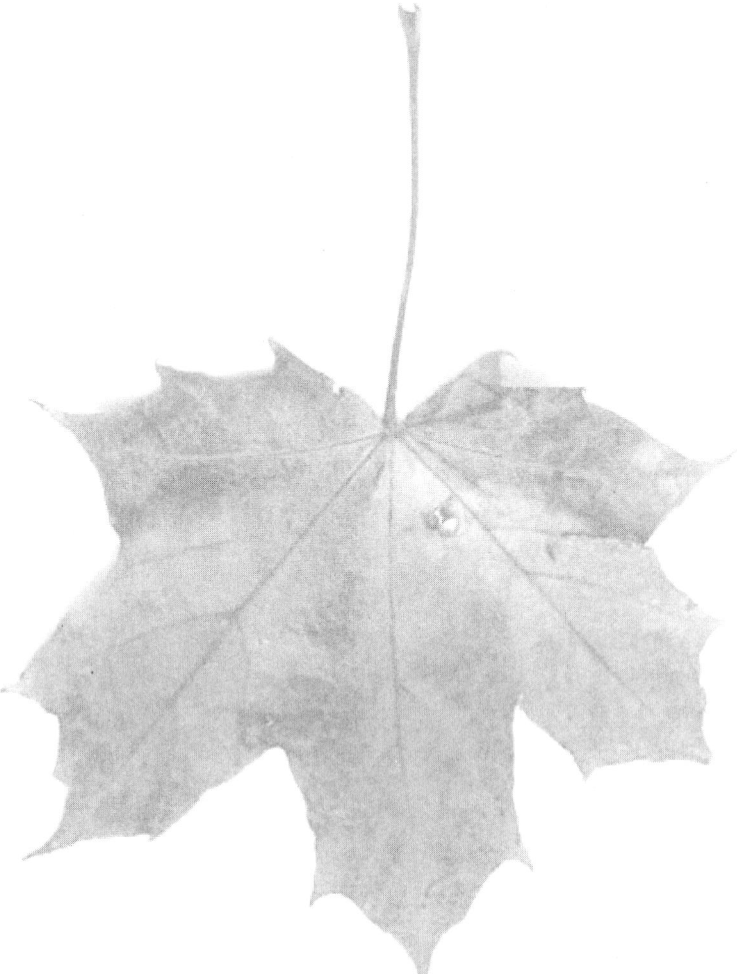

April 13, 1995

Chapter 1

Sandy Richards looked at the face staring back at her from the bathroom mirror. She had dreaded the arrival of this day for months, and now it was here. Turning forty wasn't the end of her world. At least, that is what she had been telling herself for months.

Dressed in a gray VanderCook College of Music T-shirt over green plaid pajama bottoms, she leaned closer to the mirror and touched her left temple. Was she imagining it, or were the lines around her eyes more pronounced? She took a step backward and studied herself. She was still thin and shapely where it counted, but not what anyone would call skinny. Her hair was now a washed-out blonde, a semi-successful effort to mask the gray that had begun lacing through her hair the previous year. Her youthful appearance had always been important to her. She wasn't vain. At least, she didn't think she was.

2 The Final Service

She stepped closer until her tummy once again touched the sink. Through the eyes of a child, people forty and older seemed ancient. Even her own mother looked elderly when she turned the big 4-0. A quiet chuckle caught in her throat when her thoughts turned to her music students at Walton Center Middle School. She probably reminded them of an old schoolmarm, the kind she used to watch in old Western movies. Had the inevitable occurred? Had she become old?

Her gaze dropped down to the yellow note stuck in the lower right corner of the mirror and froze there. Her father had just been admitted into Riverside Medical Center in Kankakee for testing, and she had an appointment to meet with the doctor later that afternoon to go over the results. She wasn't expecting anything too serious. Her dad was more fatigued lately than usual, and, when pressed by her mother, admitted he didn't feel like his normal antagonistic self. And he was coughing a lot.

She rolled her eyes, sighed deeply, and looked back into the mirror. Her left index finger traced the line running from the bottom corner of her nose to the end of her lip. She had never noticed how pronounced it had become. Her father's face had the same line on either side of his nose. Great, she thought. Just what I need. To look like him.

Sandy turned away from her reflection to begin the morning ritual of showering, applying makeup, dressing, and heading out to bring the joys of music to her students. Every morning she sang while getting ready for school.

On this morning, she did not.

"How's your dad, Sandy?" asked Rodger Jones. The Walton Center Middle School's assistant principal was standing at the front desk reading the morning sports page when she pulled open the door and walked into the office.

"Stubborn as ever, Rodger," she said with her lips stretched thin. She walked around her colleague to the wall of cubbyholes that doubled as mail slots. Hers was jammed with announcements, most of them useless. "Why do you ask?"

Rodger folded the paper and waited until Sandy looked over at him. "I heard he was at Riverside for tests. I'm praying for good results."

"Thank you," she replied, glancing down and pretending to study papers and envelopes clutched in her hand. "Have a nice morning," she concluded as she pushed open the door and stepped quickly down the hallway toward the band room. "Small towns," she muttered to herself.

Walton Center was the sort of place where everyone knew everyone—and all the details. The lack of privacy was bad enough, but no one was shy about asking the sorts of questions requiring answers most people didn't want others to know anything about.

Advances in communications and transportation had drawn the formerly sleepy little northern Illinois town into the gravitational clutches of Chicago. Truth be told, what was once a country village was rapidly becoming little more than a bedroom community for the Windy City. Its population was increasing, and strangers were more common here than ever. But it was still the kind of place that harbored few secrets.

Sandy paused outside her classroom to recall something she had overheard her older daughter Emiley remark to a friend: "Hey, I found your nose. It was in my business again." That pretty much summed up life in small-town middle America. The thought nearly brought a smile to her face, the hint of which just as quickly vanished. Smiles came rarely these days. When they did, Emiley and her younger sister Sarah were usually the cause.

She was about to open the door to her room when one of her students came bounding toward her, his arms outstretched for a hug. "Mrs. Richards!" It was a daily routine they both enjoyed.

"Hi Tyler! How's it going?" Sandy tousled the tow-headed boy's mop of wild hair with one hand while reaching into her pocket with the other to pull out a dollar bill. When she was sure no one was looking, she let it slip through her fingers onto the floor.

"I'm going to join band next year, Mrs. Richards. I'm going to play the drums!"

"I know, and I bet you'll be the best drummer ever!" She glanced at the floor and pretended to be surprised. "Oops, did you drop your lunch money, Tyler?"

Tyler glanced toward the crumpled dollar lying at his feet, scooped it up, shot her a wide grin, and took off down the hall.

Tracey Shirk, Walton Center's choral instructor, walked up next to Sandy and watched Tyler hoop and holler his way through the throng of students beginning to pour into the school and crowd the hallway. "That kid just always has money falling out of his pockets," she said to her best friend before lowering her voice and adding, "You can't feed them all, you know."

"Most of them feed themselves just fine," replied Sandy with a gentle nod. "With Tyler's broken home and a mom working third shift . . ."

"She usually forgets his lunch money." Tracey finished the sentence for her. "Do you think his mother ever wonders who's feeding him, or if he's even eating lunch?" she continued. "And how about those new sneakers you bought him? She has to notice."

"I don't care if she does. He's a good kid. I'm sure she works hard, and she's a single mom. It doesn't hurt to give a little help," replied Sandy.

"You're a saint, girlfriend," Tracey whispered in her ear as she slipped one arm around Sandy's shoulder and hugged her. "Not to change the subject, but . . . how's your dad doing?"

Sandy stepped away a few inches, just enough for Tracey's arm to fall away. "My father's sure getting a lot of attention today."

"People are concerned. You know that. How is he?"

Sandy took a deep breath and exhaled. "I think he's fine. He's tired. He drinks too much. He's still busy trying to start some kind of business." The words shot out like a machine gun. Cold. Rapid. Empty. "As for his other business projects, if you can call them businesses," she added before stopping herself. "Never mind," she shook her head. "I'm sure he's OK."

Tracey remained silent for a few seconds, cocking her head to one side as she always did when contemplating whether what she was about to say next was a good idea. "Well, Shadow, you need to come to grips with him. He could be gone faster than the Cubs can blow a 10-game lead in September. You two have unsettled business. You shouldn't leave it unfinished." When Sandy raised a hand to object, Tracey raised hers a tad faster, and they met palm to palm, a high-five frozen for several seconds at eye level. "We've been friends since grade school. I know you. I understand what you've gone through," continued Tracey. "I know what your family has gone through with your dad, but he's still your dad. And you only get one. And you were his shadow, Shadow." Tracey grinned at her play on words.

Sandy managed little more than a shrug and was about to speak when the school buzzer signaled it was time for the first class to begin. As she turned enter her room Tracey blurted, "Hey, I haven't forgotten."

Sandy furrowed her brow and turned to look at her friend.

"Forgotten what?

Tracey mouthed the words, "Happy birthday!" grinned, winked, and turned away.

Sandy grimaced. Why couldn't everyone just forget that nasty little fact?

Her day continued like all the others: woodwinds first period, brass next, followed by her dreaded hour with the percussionists. Of all musicians, drummers were a different breed. She would never really understand them. Today, however, the drummers knew all about her little secret, and as soon as she stepped into the room and closed the door behind her, belted out Happy Birthday as only those who make music by striking things can do.

After the rambunctious serenade fell away to fitful silence, she thanked her students, ignored their requests that she tell them her age, and continued her class as she always did. Forty-five minutes later, when she waved them into silence and told them to pack their gear, one of the drummers raised his hand.

"Yes, Elijah?"

"Were you in The Vanguard, Mrs. Richards?" he asked the question slowly, as if he wasn't exactly sure what he was asking or whether there was such a thing.

"Yes," she replied. "I was indeed. The Des Plaines Vanguard." She knew what was coming next. Everyone in the room knew. Bill Sanford, Elijah's father, had marched with The Cavaliers. The Park Ridge Cavaliers and The Des Plaines Vanguard were fierce competitors during her teenage drum and bugle corps years.

"My dad was a Cavalier."

"Yes, I know. He was playing with the enemy."

"He said they were better."

"Really? He said that?" She pursed her lips in something that wasn't a smile, but might have been mistaken for one. Usually the exchanged stopped here. None of the ways she really wanted to answer were appropriate. On this day, however, she could not stop herself. "Well, you tell your dad The Cavaliers wore green for a reason." She paused for effect. "Envy is a powerful thing."

Elijah frowned and looked at a friend. "Huh?"

The buzzer sounded.

"Saved again," she muttered under her breath as the kids scurried out of the classroom banging their sticks against the walls and slapping a beat along the white board.

Drummers.

Jazz band rehearsals passed in a bluesy haze just before lunch, and her concert band class early that afternoon marched by. When the clock hit 3:30 p.m., she made a beeline out the door straight to her car. For a moment she felt guilty, fumbling in her purse for her keys and then dropping them on the pavement as if she were a nervous petty criminal accused of doing something wrong. Music was her calling—not her vocation. There was nothing she loved more than lingering, as she nearly always did, in the band room with some of her favorite students. There, Sandy would spend an hour or more strumming her guitar, singing with her "kids," and teaching them everything from music theory and harmonies to why the Beatles were better than the Stones. But not today.

Sandy was unlocking her blue Dodge Caravan when a woman's voice shouted, "Mrs. Richards!" She turned to her right and watched as a woman she did not know walked quickly toward her from two rows away. "Hi, I'm Marilou Sanford, Elijah's mom," she said rather breathlessly when she stepped within a few feet of Sandy, using one hand to brush back the long strands of raven hair that had fallen across her cheek. "He is one of your percussion students. I think you knew my husband Bill years ago."

"Sure, hello, Mrs. Sanford," replied Sandy, who marveled at the woman's youthful appearance. How could she be that young and fit and have a teenaged son Elijah's age? Sandy prepared herself for what was coming next. Parents don't chase teachers down in the parking lot to extol their virtues in the classroom. The flippant exchange she had with Elijah about The Cavaliers and The Vanguard leapt to mind. "What can I do for you?"

Marilou hesitated, smiled, and then bit her lip before replying, "I—we—my husband and I, and of course, Elijah . . . just wanted you to know—our family is praying for you."

Sandy tilted her head back slightly and raised her eyebrows. "Praying? For me?"

"I know how close I am to my daddy, and we heard yours is in for testing," she continued. "We're praying God will place his healing hand on him and make him healthy again. And that He will pull you close and relieve your anxiety regarding your daddy's health."

Daddy. Sandy caught a trace of a Southern accent and recalled something about Elijah's mom being from Alabama. "Yes, well. Thank you, but . . ."

"And that God uses this challenge with your daddy's health to pull you both closer to Him."

"My daddy," Sandy stumbled on the word. "Right, well..." She really didn't know what to say. She shifted the books she was carrying from her left arm to her right and stood ramrod straight, her rigid body language screaming her discomfort to anyone paying attention. "Thank you, Mrs. Sanford, but my father is fine. He's like a tank. He's old and battered, mostly from self-abuse, but I'm sure he'll be okay." She flashed a fake grin. "If I were you, I wouldn't waste prayers on Tom Loucks."

For an uncomfortable moment Elijah's mother stared without replying or moving, processing the chill buried within Sandy's response. "Mrs. Richards," she began softly, "prayers are never wasted. God hears them. All of them."

"I'm sure he does."

"And He can use all things for His good purpose."

"Yes, well, thank you. I appreciate your concern, but I have to run."

Sandy climbed into her Caravan and drove away, glancing into the rearview mirror to catch a final glimpse of Elijah's mom, mouth agape as she drove away. Her facial features spoke volumes: how could her son's teacher be so cold and rude? When she caught her own reflection Sandy quickly looked away. The bags under her eyes were dark and pronounced. Stifling back a sob, she eased her Caravan to the side of the road, shifted into park, and flipped down her visor to study her face in the mirror. It was all she could do to keep from crying. "Am I depressed?" she thought, looking deeply into her own eyes as if they might hold the answer. "What is wrong with me?" she asked aloud. She was never rude or short with anyone, let alone a student's parent, but something had changed. And this was the first time she fully recognized it.

Sandy dabbed a white Kleenex against the tears gathering in her eyes and blew her nose. When she glanced at her watch and realized the time, she eased her way back into traffic, heading out Route 102 toward Kankakee. It was time to meet Tom Loucks' doctor.

She arrived at Riverside Medical Center hoping to secure a parking place close to the entrance. Finding none, she pulled into the adjacent lot and walked the long path to the building housing the physicians' offices. "Why can't they just tell me the results over the phone?" she mumbled aloud as she stepped around an elderly woman heading in the same direction.

"What my dear?" asked the woman. Sandy waved the question away without breaking stride, passing through the automatic doors to stand in front of the tall black sign with white lettering on the lobby wall boasting an over-sized list of physician names. Her frustration level mounted when she realized the names were organized by floor rather than alphabetically. Her father's doctor, Andrew Albright, MD, was on the fourth floor.

"My name is Sandy Richards," she said once inside the office. "I'm here to see Doctor Albright about my dad's test. His name is Tom Loucks."

"Yes, Mrs. Richards, the doctor is waiting for you," answered the young receptionist. "You can go inside." She gestured toward a door just beyond the desk.

"Waiting for me?" she said in surprise, and more loudly than she had intended. "Since when do doctors wait for patients?"

"The doctor will see you now, Mrs. Richards. He is right through there."

Sandy stepped toward the door, which opened on cue to reveal a nurse, who escorted her down a long hallway to an office at the end. "Mrs. Richards to see you, Doctor Albright."

"Good afternoon, Mrs. Richards," said the doctor, who stood from behind his desk and extended his hand. Sandy shook it briefly. "Please, have a seat," he continued, gesturing toward a faux burgundy leather wingback chair facing his own desk. With his full head of hair, soft round face, and white medical coat, he looked strikingly like Doogie Howser. "Great," she thought as she settled into the chair.

Dr. Albright pulled his own chair up, rested his arms on his desk, and laced his fingers together. His lips were pursed, tightly. "Thank you for coming, Mrs. Richards," He sighed before continuing. "I am sorry your mother wasn't able to make it, but your dad authorized for me to speak with you." He paused to clear his throat. "This is hard, so I'll get right to the point. Your father has lung cancer. I've already brought in another colleague for a second opinion."

It took her a moment to process the full extent of the words. Several seconds passed in uncomfortable silence. "What's the prognosis?"

"Your father has stage four lung cancer. It has already spread to his liver and to his brain." His words rushed together like one lengthy syllable, few of them making any sense to her. "Because of the type of cancer, how far it has progressed, and where it's moving through his body . . ." He stopped long enough to slide a box of tissue from the distant corner of his oversized desk to within Sandy's reach. "It's inoperable, Mrs. Richards. There is really nothing we can do for your father other than keep him as comfortable as possible. I am very sorry." His slight shrug coupled with the painfully serious look on his face went hand in hand with his prognosis.

"It's inoperable." The words reverberated in her head—six syllables as loud and irritating as cymbal crashes, soon reduced to five. Inoperable. A wave of dizziness swept over her and she gripped the arms of the chair to steady herself.

Lingering silence pervaded the room. "Okay," she finally replied. "You can't operate. How will you treat him?"

Dr. Albright cleared his throat once more. "Well, as I said, there is no treatment, per se. We will certainly try to make him as comfortable as possible." He paused a moment. "Mrs. Richards, your father has been—I'm unsure of the precise word—ignoring, hiding, masking his condition for a long time."

"Comfortable," she repeated staring vacantly at the wall of medical reference books lining the shelves behind him.

"What I'm trying to communicate is that your dad doesn't just have stage four cancer. He is at the end of stage four. Frankly, I have no idea how he has been able to hide the pain he must be experiencing. We have never seen anything quite like it."

The doctor caught her stare and looked into her eyes, his gaze kindly, understanding. He recognized her inability to accept reality. He had seen it before, dozens of times. "Mrs. Richards, are there any other family members here with you? Or anyone else we should talk with? A husband, a sibling, perhaps?"

"I understand," came her whispered non-reply. Her words were slow. Measured. "I don't need . . . anyone. You just said my . . . father . . . is dying." She paused, folded her arms across her chest, and stood up from the chair—ramrod straight. "I will take him home." It sounded more like a command than a simple statement.

"Home?" Sandy's reaction didn't really surprise Dr. Albright. Everyone reacted differently to news like this. "Isn't there someone I can call?" he asked as he followed her lead and stood up. "Perhaps your mother? You shouldn't be alone."

"I'm the only one who can handle this," she replied.

"I think perhaps your mom . . ."

Sandy cut him off mid-sentence. "My mom's health isn't up to it, or she would be here." Her voice trailed off before she haltingly continued. "I know this is all on my shoulders, but I'm not ... I'm not sure what to do next. What do I do once I take him home?"

The doctor gestured toward her chair, and together they sat back down. "Your father is too frail and too sick to go home." Sandy's eyes opened wide, as if comprehending for the first time just how ill her dad really was. "Often patients come in looking relatively healthy on the outside," he continued, "but once they get the diagnosis their bodies quickly catch up with reality. He needs to be in a nursing facility and, in my opinion, receiving hospice care. Do you know what hospice is?" She nodded slowly but didn't respond.

"Is there someone I can call, Mrs. Richards?"

She shook her head. "No. I just need to figure out how to tell my mom. That's all. For me, that will be the hardest part of all of this. I'll figure out the rest."

"We will keep your dad here and coordinate hospice care with you," said Dr. Albright as he stood and walked out from behind his desk. "At this point there is nothing you need to do in that regard, and we will be in touch with you for paperwork and other information."

"Thank you, doctor." She turned to leave, but stopped and asked, "How long does he have?"

He shook his head. "We can never determine with any great accuracy. It could be a few weeks, a month." He shrugged. "He could have several months. It's hard to predict with real certainty."

"Several months," she repeated as she walked toward the door.

Chapter 2

"How did your mom take the news?" Steve asked his wife of seventeen years, as they pulled back the comforter and readied for bed.

"It was the hardest thing I've ever had to tell anyone." Sandy sat down and pushed a lock of hair behind her left ear with one hand while slowing brushing her hair with the other. "I could tell by the look on mother's face. She already knew what I was going to say."

"You should have called me. I should have been there."

"I'm always surprised by mom's internal strength," continued Sandy. "She cried, but only for a minute or two. Then she started calling my brothers, other relatives, a few old friends." She turned to fluff her pillow. "Mother never loses control. You know that."

"Her strength comes from her faith," offered Steve.

Sandy stopped brushing and turned to look at her husband. "Faith in what?" she spat, pointing the brush at him like a knife. "Haven't we progressed beyond believing in an all-knowing, all-seeing wizard? I think Toto pulled back that curtain." Her tone was cold, her words razor sharp. "My dad's a drunk and has been an embarrassment to the family for years. Mom may be relieved when the time comes." When Steve didn't reply, Sandy turned her back to him and began brushing her hair once more, her strokes fast and almost manic in their intensity.

Steve sighed and put her hand on his wife's shoulder. The brushing stopped immediately, but she didn't turn around to face him. "I understand, Sandy," he began tentatively, knowing he was tiptoeing through an emotional minefield. "What we see is always dependent upon where we stand. I love your dad. He's the only father I've ever known. He's been good to me. Trust me when I tell you that as a fatherless kid, a drunk father is better than no father at all . . ." Steve's voice broke.

Sandy turned back to look at Steve. She still held her brush, but was no longer wielding it like a weapon. "You have never talked about this before," she whispered.

"Your dad never left you," he continued. "My dad never looked back as he walked out the door. I have no idea where he went or even where he is today. I don't even know if he's alive. He doesn't care about what I'm doing or where I am." He glanced at the glass of red wine on Sandy's nightstand. "And your dad suffers from an addiction to alcohol. Mine didn't have that excuse."

"So what's your point?"

"It all started when your dad left his job at the plant and started his business. He told me he needed his beer at night to relax. I can't judge him." He paused before his voice took on a steely tone that matched the passion in his eyes. "I won't judge him."

"Then don't judge me," Sandy snapped, interpreting his words as an accusation about her own behavior. She glared at him when his glance slowly returned to rest on her wine glass. "Oh, I get it," she said with deep sarcasm. "I don't have to have this wine." She picked up the glass and studied the ruby Pinot Noir for a moment. "I enjoy it. But I don't need it. Besides, it's good for my heart. And I have never embarrassed you or the kids."

"No you haven't," he answered, "but I wasn't insinuating anything. I just think you've always been too harsh on the old guy. He's your dad. At least you have one. There must have been good times with your father, Sandy. I mean, the old-timers around town still call you 'Shadow.' According to them, wherever Tom went, you were always right there by his side. You were daddy's little girl—"

"Once," she said, cutting him off mid-sentence. "A long time ago." She put the brush down and slid between the sheets, settled back against her pillows and the headboard, "He's not your father, Steve. You didn't grow up with him. It's easy for you to be so nonchalant about what he's done to all of us."

Steve climbed into bed next to her. "True enough," he admitted. He's a World War II vet. In my book, that earns him hero status. He married your mom and never left her side. His service to his country and devotion to his family says a lot. He raised you into the woman you've become and the woman I love." He stopped for her to respond. When she remained silent, he continued. "Remember, he's the one who allowed you to join that drum and bugley thing you love. He's the guy who worked all day, then drove you seventy miles round trip to rehearsals. He couldn't have been that bad."

"That bugley thing?" She mocked his words, shaking her head. Steve had never understood her relationship with The Vanguard. "If you were in The Vanguard, no explanation is necessary. If you weren't, no explanation is possible." She looked at her glass of wine, raising it so the light reflected through the rich color. "And that's too bad," she added, anxious to change the subject." You would have been pretty cute in that red cadet uniform."

While Steve chuckled, Sandy sat upright in bed. "Get this. A mother of one of my students stopped me in the parking lot today. She told me she was praying for me." She paused to take a long sip. "Praying. It was horribly uncomfortable. I'm afraid I was rude."

"You?" he replied with obvious surprise evident in his features. "I've never seen you be rude to anyone but me." He laughed, but he did so alone. "Sandy, what's gotten into you lately?"

She ignored Steve's question. "It's all left to me."

"What's left to you?"

"The mess!" She emptied what was left in her glass, put it on the nightstand, and turned back to her husband. "There's more than two decades of garbage stored in that filthy old warehouse he calls a pole barn. Who is going to go through all that crap? Mom? My out-of-state brothers? Of course not. It will be me."

Now it was Steve's turn to sit up. "Sandy, I'll help you! I can—"

She cut him off again. "You don't have time, Steve, and this is not a weekend project! It will take weeks or longer to sort through that disgusting place. My entire summer vacation will be spent trying to figure out what is worth keeping and what needs to be tossed." The more she spoke, the louder and angrier she became. "You know what? I think he did this to me on purpose. He ruined my birthday, and now he's going to ruin my summer." Her eyes drilled into Steve's stunned gaze. "Tom Loucks. World War Two hero and Father of the Year."

"Come on Sandy, that's crazy. You don't mean that."

"I sure do!" Her voice ticked up another notch as the tempo of her speech increased. "So now he dies and leaves his barn full of worthless crap, stacked floor to ceiling. Mom told me his final request was that I clean it up. Me! No one else! She made me promise! And what did he think would happen to all that stacked up garbage?"

When Steve didn't immediately answer, Sandy threw one pillow on the floor, punched down her remaining pillow, and rolled away from her husband.

"Good night, Sandy," he whispered as he turned off the lamp. "I don't know what to tell you. I'm sorry this all happened on your birthday."

The only reply was the ticking clock on his nightstand.

Chapter 3

Sandy picked up the receiver on the fourth ring and managed a mumbled, "Hello?" with a simultaneous glance at the clock. It was nearly midnight.

"Mrs. Richards? Sandy Richards?" It was a female voice, older and authoritative.

"This is Sandy. Who's calling?" she replied.

"I am so sorry to bother you at this hour. This is Ann Puleo. I'm an RN and nightshift floor supervisor at the Kankakee River Valley Hospice Center."

Sandy sat up in bed, now wide awake. "What's wrong?"

"Your father's breathing has become very labored and his heart rate is irregular, Mrs. Richards." She paused before continuing. "Your father is failing and it might be best for you and your family to come, quickly."

Sandy and Steve dressed, called and picked up Sandy's mom, and drove the twenty miles to the hospice facility within an hour of receiving the call. It was too late. Less than two weeks after his diagnosis, Thomas John Loucks was gone.

Sandy consoled her distraught mother for nearly thirty minutes without shedding a tear of her own.

"He didn't even have the common courtesy to wait until we arrived," Sandy replied when Steve asked her how she felt a few hours later when they arrived back home. "He just left without saying good-bye. I don't care about me. But he didn't wait for Mom."

Chapter 4

The outpouring of respect for the man Sandy had grown to disrespect both confused and angered her.

She was in the process of climbing into a black limousine when she stopped to survey the long line of cars stacked up like horizontal dominos behind it. "I can't believe all these people," she whispered to Steve before sliding inside next to her mother.

Her words were meant for her husband's ears only, but her mother's hearing was better than she had thought. A small white-gloved hand came to rest upon her arm. "These people respected and loved your father, Sandy. I'm well aware of how you feel—but you are wrong." Dorothy Loucks stared out the window for several seconds as if counting to ten to temper the words to follow. "I only wish you could see your dad as I saw him."

"I'm sorry, Mom. I didn't mean any disrespect—"

"No, Sandy, you never do," her mother cut in. "The man in that casket supported this family and helped me raise our three children. He always made sure that none of us—especially you—ever wanted for anything."

"I know, mom, I was—."

Her mother cut her off a second time, her voice taking on an unaccustomed agitated tone. "Who clothed you? Who made sure you got a good education? My goodness, who drove you seventy-miles, round trip to Vanguard rehearsals until you were old enough to drive yourself?"

Sandy remained silent.

"But what, Sandy?" Her mother asked sharply. "I am sure there is a 'but' about to come out of your mouth." Dorothy barely paused to take a breath before continuing. "You never had to pay off a student loan. Who moved you out of your dorm and into your first apartment? And who paid your rent until you started your first job?"

Sandy looked at her mom, who locked her eyes on her daughter and refused to let go.

"From the moment you were born that man loved you. No, that's not true. He was crazy about you even before you were born. Every night before he went to sleep, he talked to you as you grew inside me. He told you stories. He sang to you. When you were born, no man was ever happier to have a daughter. He rocked you, cared for, and sang to you. Why, until you were twelve, you wouldn't respond to your own name. You only answered to Shadow. Wherever your father was, his shadow was right there with him. You loved that nickname—Shadow—and so did he. Do you remember?"

When Sandy nodded, Dorothy took a breath and continued. "Your father . . . why, he cherished you!" The last words caught in her mouth. She stopped a moment, wiped an eye with her tissue, and continued. "You changed his life. Now he's gone, and you seem to have no idea who he was, or how much he adored you. And that's why he wants *you* to clean the barn. And don't you dare forget your promise to do so."

It was then her mother, the good and faithful wife who had remained by her husband's side for forty-nine years, began to sob.

Sandy swallowed hard but was unable to stop the stream of unexpected tears flowing down her own cheeks. "I'm sorry, Mom."

Her mother lifted her gloved hand from Sandy's arm and held it up, palm out, in a gesture that could only be interpreted as stop!

Steve reached in the seatback pocket in front of him for a Kleenex while Sandy smoothed non-existent wrinkles from her blue skirt.

The black hearse in front of them slowed and came to a stop, triggering a similar chain reaction behind it that extended the length of several city blocks. Steve reached across his wife and gently cupped his mother-in-law's hand with his own, using his other to hold one of Sandy's empty hands. "We love you mom. And we loved Tom. In so many ways he was my father, too."

The awkward silence was interrupted when a crisply attired Marine officer in his dress blues approached the limousine and tapped lightly on the side window. It was only when Steve lowered the window that he noticed several medals pinned to his chest. The tall officer leaned slightly into the open window. His eyes met those of each passenger until they came to rest upon Mrs. Loucks.

"Ma'am. I'm Captain John McClellan. It's my honor and privilege to be your escort." His voice was solemn, formal, deep, and melodious. The Marine paused a moment before opening the door and extending his white-gloved hand to assist Sergeant Tom Loucks' widow in exiting the limo.

"I'm sorry—did you say captain?" she asked with a confused look on her face.

"Yes, Ma'am."

"Captain McClellan, my husband was in the army."

The Marine extended his bent arm. "Yes, ma'am. I'm taking you to meet Captain Frank Pamper. He's a soldier like your husband. Would you mind walking just a short distance with me?"

Dorothy nodded approvingly, took his arm, and together they began a slow walk toward the cemetery, her back almost as straight and rigid as the Marine officer's. Sandy and Steve followed behind them.

They walked a short distance before stopping next to another officer. "Mrs. Thomas John Loucks," announced Captain McClellan, "this is Captain Frank Pamper, United States Army, Ma'am."

"Mrs. Loucks," responded Captain Pamper with the firmness and clarity one would expect at a military funeral. Like Captain McClellan, he wore the dress uniform of his branch of service. "We're here today to honor your husband and pay tribute to his service to our country. Please allow me to escort you to your seat." He offered Dorothy his crooked arm for support. Turning to Sandy, Steve, and the rest of their family, he added, "Please follow us."

With the six pallbearers carrying the casket just to their front, Captain Pamper led them to chairs upholstered in burgundy velvet and reserved for immediate family only. Once they were seated, Steve and the girls stood directly behind Sandy and her mom.

"Please be seated," said the Loucks' family pastor as he surveyed the large crowd with what could only be described as a pleased look on his face. "God of Grace and Glory," he began,

> we remember before You today, our brother, Thomas John Loucks, husband, father, grandfather, friend, businessman, and soldier. We thank you for giving Tom to us to know and to love as a companion in our earthly pilgrimage. In Your boundless compassion, console those of us who mourn. Give us faith to see that death has been swallowed up by the cross and the resurrection of Jesus Christ. Be

with Tom's family. Give them the peace and comfort through Your assurance that Tom is now with You and that he is free of the stresses and pressures of this life. In the name of Your Son, our Savior, Jesus Christ. Amen.

The pastor cleared his throat to dislodge the lump that had formed there. "It is fitting that today, Tom, our dear friend and family member, is honored for his service to our country," he began. "A member of the World War II generation, he rose to the occasion, answered the call of his country, and served bravely and honorably." The pastor's gaze scanned the entire gathering before settling upon Sandy. "I knew Tom well. Very well. Few will ever understand the price he paid in defense of his country. Very few."

The Walton Center American Legion Honor Guard of seven men ranging from fifty to eighty years of age snapped to attention. When the moment arrived, their rifles snapped to their shoulders in unison.

"Fire!" Sandy's body jerked at the eruption of the first volley.

"Fire!" the second volley seemed much louder, and the third louder still.

The members of the Honor Guard carefully removed the flag from the casket, folded it, and once formed into the ceremonial triangle, handed the sacred banner to Captain Pamper. The captain tucked the flag against his waist, stepped toward the family, and knelt on one knee in front of the widow.

"Mrs. Loucks," he began, "this flag is presented on behalf of a grateful nation and the United States Army. Please accept this flag that draped your husband's casket as a symbol of appreciation for the honorable and faithful service of Sergeant Thomas John Loucks."

Dorothy, her cheeks awash in tears, cradled the flag in her arms and pulled it close. "God bless you, ma'am." The captain nodded his respects to the rest of the family, turned smartly, and walked away.

When a single tear leaked out of Sandy's right eye and began tracing its way through her makeup, a sudden rush of emotion welled up inside her chest. She reached back for Steve's hand. As always, he was there for her.

A lone bugler sounded the haunting melody of Taps. He held the last of the two dozen notes for several seconds. It took a moment for its echo to fade away. Silence drifted once more over the cemetery.

"God bless you all," the pastor concluded. "The family has asked you to join them at the church hall where a luncheon has been prepared. On behalf of the family and our departed friend Tom, thank you for joining us today."

Chapter 5

The alarm sounded at 6:00 a.m., lifting Sandy out of a deep sleep into the arms of the first morning of summer vacation. She had no intention of sleeping in. Today was a work day, and she would spend it in her father's pole barn.

The unmistakable scent of frying bacon filled the bedroom. She breathed deeply and dressed quietly, pulling on a pair of blue denim shorts before slipping a white short-sleeved T-shirt trimmed with bright red piping over her head. She glanced in the mirror at the red and black shield logo with the word Vanguard strategically placed as if it were over her heart. The brush she ran through her hair several times removed the tangles. What she could not shake free was her mother's heated reminder from three weeks earlier that it was her father who always made the long drives to and from her Vanguard rehearsals. Digging through her top drawer, she settled on a pair of white athletic socks, laced up her worn red and black running shoes, and joined Steve in the kitchen.

"You're up early for a Monday, Steve," she said reaching for the coffee pot.

"Thought I'd make my girl a good breakfast to kick off her summer." He pulled her close and kissed her forehead before turning the thick bacon strips sizzling in the black iron skillet.

"Thanks," she replied, "but I really need to get started—and get this over." Without so much as a glance over her shoulder, she filled her mug and headed out the door.

"It's nothing but a saggy old barn, that's all it is," Sandy muttered to herself before turning off the engine of her Caravan. She remained in the driver's seat, studying the shabby wooden structure her family generously referred to as a pole barn. Her eyes took in the warped boards and partially rotted framing of the building that would serve as her summer prison. In happier days, a little girl had helped her dad slap two coats of paint on it. Cracks now lined the 2 x 6 horizontal side boards, and what little paint remained had faded into a nondescript color no one would now describe as yellow. Age catches up with everything, she thought. The grass around the structure, always kept neat and trimmed in the past, had been replaced by a knee-high crop of weeds. Even the fissures in the cracked asphalt drive were full of them.

Sandy climbed out of the minivan, shut the door, and sighed deeply. The dilapidated wooden sign on the front corner of the building revealed fourteen faded letters in two words: "Loucks Ventures." As if on cue, a wooden shingle slid off the roof and fell on the asphalt a few feet in front of her and directly in front of the sign.

"Ventures. Yeah, right." The short burst of laughter sounded hollow even to her. There was no way to get out of the work waiting for her inside. A half-dozen slow steps carried her to the rotten front door. She inserted the key and stopped short. How many times had she and her father walked through this door holding hands? She shook the memory back into the past, eased the door aside, and entered the cavernous room.

The building was already old when her father bought it more than three decades earlier. He had no particular purpose in mind for the structure, but the price was right, he explained to both his wife and his daughter, and "a man can always use a place to store stuff."

And use it he did.

Sandy flipped the main light switch only to discover most of the bulbs were burned out. The few that remained cast just enough light to illuminate the general nature of the task confronting her. For thirty years Tom Loucks had been stuffing the large building from floor to ceiling with items he simply could not bring himself to throw away. They included nearly everything imaginable, from wooden and cardboard boxes, to bags, old appliances, books, file cabinets, furniture, dishes, tools, mason jars full of nuts and bolts, and who knew what else—all the random items a person accumulates over a lifetime. Rumor had it there was even a car buried in here somewhere, the make and model of which depended upon the person doing the telling. One thing was certain, thought Sandy as she eased her way deeper into the barn. It would take all summer—and maybe longer—to sort through this place.

Sandy drew a deep breath and took a step back as if she'd been assaulted. The stench of mold and rot was stronger than she had expected. She swallowed to stifle the frustration welling up inside her before kicking the nearest box in disgust. Then she kicked it again so hard her foot crashed through it. "Calm yourself, girl," she said aloud. She had work to do, and anger wouldn't get the job done. But a plan would, and she needed to settle on one.

She scanned mound after mound of old boxes and black plastic bags, all bulging with contents unknown. "One box at a time . . . one bag at a time." She could do this. One stack at a time. She looked up and realized she would need a twenty-foot ladder just to reach the top of some of these mountains of junk.

Sandy offered to have it all hauled away, but her mother wouldn't hear of it. "There are things your father treasured buried away in that building!" she scolded. "He wasn't crazy, Sandy. He only saved what needed saving, and there are lots of valuable antiques and other things in there." The elephant in the room rarely acknowledged, and never fully explored, was the mountain of debt her father had left behind. "Promise me you will look through everything," she pleaded. "Promise me."

"I'll do it for you, mom. Yes, I promise."

"I promise." The words echoed in the barn even though they existed only in her head.

"I hate you, Tom Loucks, for leaving this to me!" For years, Sandy had referred to her father as either Tom or "my mother's husband." Even his death hadn't changed that barb of disrespect.

And so the daughter, faithful to her mother, was left with the daunting task of opening each box and every bag, looking at every item, and determining what could or should be saved or sold. She decided to attack the stack of boxes off to her right and move down the length of the west side of the barn, one pile at a time. But without the ladder, how could she begin?

She put a hand out and pushed the stack gently. It wavered. With no concern for their contents, and without much if any thought, she lowered her shoulder like a Walton Center High School linebacker and smashed into the cardboard tower. The first tower of boxes she assaulted, however, was reinforced from behind with other stacks of similar boxes. She watched in dismay and as the stack she had rammed with her left shoulder, as if in slow motion, toppled toward her. She tried to jump out of the way but fell to the floor as the boxes fell all around her.

Stunned but uninjured, and still sprawled on the floor, she clawed her way back a few feet in case any other boxes decided to come down. None did. She reached over to her left and shook the nearest box. Next, she extended her foot, tapped another, and gave it a kick. The box slid several feet. They were much lighter than she expected. Frowning now, she twisted and pushed a third box with her foot with the same result. Sandy scrambled closer and pulled at the faded brittle tape sealing it.

"Leaves! Leaves?" She looked up as if expecting her father to be in the rafters above her. "You saved tree leaves?" She shoved her hands into the box, grabbed a handful of the moldy reddish brown leaves, and threw them as hard as she was able. "What was wrong with you, Tom Loucks? Were you absolutely nuts?" Screaming, she picked up the box and hoisted it above her head. She was about to throw it when a voice interrupted her.

"Excuse me, ma'am?"

It was a male voice coming from the doorway. "Are you okay?"

Still holding the box, Sandy swiveled her head to find a handsome young man standing a few feet inside the building. He stood about six feet tall, with light, closely cropped brown hair and penetrating brown eyes. His olive-colored T-shirt, snug perhaps to highlight his fit body, was tucked into a pair of khaki pants that were in turn tucked into a pair of black boots.

"Ma'am?" Her quick head toss and roll of her eyes signaled her level of displeasure. At least she hoped it did. "Did you really just call me ma'am?"

The stranger smiled. "Would you prefer I call you miss?" She met his smile with a silent glare. "I heard a scream," he continued. "I didn't mean to startle you or intrude. I was afraid you were in danger."

"And you came to save me?" she said with as much sarcasm as she could muster.

The stranger nodded. "If necessary, yes." His eyes wandered slowly upward from her face to well above her head. "You're not going to throw that at me, are you?"

Only then did Sandy remember she was still holding, arms fully extended, a filthy cardboard box. When it dawned on her how silly she must look, she dropped it as if it had suddenly overheated. Not knowing what to do with her hands, she attached them firmly to her hips.

"I'll take that as a no," he grinned. "So . . . do you?"

Her eyebrows knit together as she cocked her head at the mysterious visitor. The loud sigh she blew ruffled the hair framing her face. "Do I what?"

"Need saving."

She averted her eyes as if she'd just spotted something interesting on the filthy floor. Her features visibly softened. "Only from myself, apparently," she whispered.

"How can I help?"

"You? You can't help."

"How do you know?"

"My mother's husband died. He left all this for me to sort through, dispose of, and clean up. Not to mention he left her with large debts. I'm hoping to find things of value to sell—to help her. I don't think that's going to happen, though. So . . . I'm a little angry, and I guess just indulging in a little pity party."

"You said he was your 'mother's husband.' I take that to mean he was your step-father?" asked the stranger.

She looked away for a quick moment for returning to meet his gaze. "He was my biological father."

"I see," he replied. "Why are you so angry?"

"What business is it of yours?" she asked, lifting her hands from her hips to turn her palms face-up. The stranger simply looked at her without answering. "Why do you think?" she finally replied, waving her arms toward the stacks of boxes, bags, cabinets, and other countless items crammed into the barn. "He left all this for me to deal with. I have no idea why he did this to me."

Instead of leaving, as Sandy believed he would, the stranger asked, "Do you mind if I sit for a few moments?" He pointed to a dust-covered folding chair leaning against the front wall.

"Why would you?" she asked. "I didn't scream because I was in trouble, and I don't need your help." Once again he remained silent, locking his deep brown eyes onto hers. There was something about his stare that was both unsettling and comforting at the same time. "Sure. Pull up a chair," replied Sandy as she wiped her dusty hands on her denim shorts. "This should be quite a show. You can watch me have a total meltdown while I dig through thirty-plus years of garbage." Who was this guy and why was he here?

The stranger walked into the shadows and unfolded the rusty brown chair, sat down, and leaned forward resting his elbows on his knees. "What did you mean when you said your dad 'did this' to you?" The question was sincerely asked, as if he really wanted to understand.

"Well, I didn't do this to myself," she snapped back, letting her sarcasm get the best of her once more. "I don't know," she added. "Apparently, God hates me."

At that, the stranger's eyebrows shot up, and he scratched one side of his head before resting his chin in the palm of his right hand. "God hates you?"

"If there really is a God, yeah, probably." Sandy wiped a bit of cobweb off one eyebrow before continuing. "If you're going to repeat everything I say, I may ask you to leave. Right now, I can't stand being around me, and I certainly don't want to listen to some stranger repeat all the awful things I'm saying. To go back to your question, if He exists, I am not one of His favorites. Would you do this to someone you love?"

"So . . . you believe your father and God are co-conspirators working against you? They left this barn full of stuff because"—he paused, turning his hands over—"they hate you?" The stranger adjusted his chair. "This should be interesting."

"Interesting?"

The man laughed. "Are you going to start repeating me now?"

"Are you staying?"

"Would you deny me a place to rest after my willingness to rescue you from danger?" he asked, his expression changing from inquisitive to mischievous in the space of a second.

"No, of course not," replied Sandy. Is he flirting with me? she wondered. "What was your name again?"

"Again?" He flashed another wide grin. "I don't believe I've told you. Just call me Sam."

"Sam," she repeated as she inspected him from head to foot. He looked a few years younger, she thought. He was also handsome, but was missing a small clump of hair on the side of his head.

"And you're Sandy."

Now it was her turn to be surprised. "And I'm sure I never mentioned my name," she said, taking an involuntary step backward as she folded her arms across her chest. "How do you know my name?"

"Small town," he said with a broad smile.

"Under different circumstances, I'm sure it would be a pleasure to meet you, but I have work to do," she added, standing ramrod straight and taking a step toward him. "I only have this summer to clean up this fabulous inheritance."

"Inheritance is an interesting word," continued Sam, ignoring what was obviously intended to be his dismissal. "What's the hurry?"

"It's a small town, right?" When Sam nodded slowly, she added, "Then you must know I'm a teacher, and teachers have the summer off. If I wanted to clean or pick up something, I could do that at home. Instead . . . here I am."

Once again Sam remained silent, tilting his head slightly as he looked at her.

"You must think I'm rude and ungrateful," added Sandy quickly. "I'm really not." She paused. Was that still true? "At least I didn't use to be . . ."

"So what changed?"

"Look," she answered, her tone one of complete exasperation. "I don't have time to give you all the gruesome details of my life. I have a lot of work to do. So if you don't mind . . ." Sandy gestured toward the barn door.

Sam remained right where he was sitting and ignored her invitation to leave. "I am still waiting to hear why you think your dad did this to you, and why you think God hates you."

"How can that be unclear to you?" she asked incredulously. "You do see all this garbage, right? My father spent years collecting it, and he knew mom was not well enough to go through it. He knew my brothers lived out of state. He knew my husband was always swamped at work." Every word brought the emotions hiding deep inside her welling closer to the surface. She used her dusty thumb to wipe away an unexpected tear. "Who else was going to do this other than me?"

"I think I see your point," replied Sam. "So, what's your plan?" he asked, looking around at the various stacks surrounding them. "Because you're going to need one."

No kidding, she thought. "Well, it's pretty obvious, right? I need to start in one spot and go through every container, every bag, every box, every file cabinet, everything . . . and determine what has value and what doesn't."

"By the look of things," he replied, standing up and turning around slowly in a circle to view the entire barn, "that could take you all summer." He sat once more, the mischievous grin back in place.

She twisted her face into something resembling a crooked smile. "Good one."

"So was your dad—what do they call those folks? A hoarder?"

"I suppose so. Look, why would he save all his garbage?" she asked, gesturing toward the boxes nearest her feet. "Look at what I just found. Leaves. In every box I've opened so far." She kicked one, and it tumbled several feet. "See what I mean? It might as well be empty. But he took the time to jam it with leaves, tape it shut, and stack it here." She paused a moment before lowering her voice. "My greatest fear is that I will waste my entire summer combing through boxes and bags and find nothing but a virtual forest—without the trees."

If she was hoping Sam would provide her with insight as to why any man would do such a thing, she was disappointed. He returned her gaze with a look of sympathetic understanding, but without a single word of wisdom.

Sandy turned away from the stranger, grabbed the nearest box, used her nail to slice through the rotting tape, and found nothing but leaves. She pushed it aside. Another box, this one taller and longer looked more promising. She repeated the process with the same result. She shoved it next to the other open container. A third try yielded the same result.

"I don't think your dad did this to you, Sandy. And I'm certain God does not hate you."

At that, she spun around as fast as she could and took two quick strides toward the chair, stopping just three feet away. "Oh, really?" she spat, her voice rising with emotion. "Then why am I here surrounded by all this?"

Sam remained seated and didn't blink an eye. "Sometimes things just happen," he offered. "You may never know why. People can be unpredictable. Life is unpredictable. Sometimes events we think are catastrophic are actually blessings in disguise. We never know until they play out. And how they play out, well, that is partially dependent upon how we respond to them."

"How we respond? Are you kidding me?" she laughed. "Exactly how am I supposed to respond to this building full of worthless stuff that, according to the World of Sam, could be a blessing to someone? I'm sure it's not a blessing to me."

"Things are rarely as they appear on the surface."

"Knowing Tom Loucks, all of this is exactly what I expected," she said, turning to walk back to the stack where she left off. She opened another box. "Ah, this is new!" she exclaimed. "Leaves!" She ripped open another. "Wow, look! More leaves." She pulled down a large black garbage bag and tore open one side to let the dry foliage fall to the ground at her feet.

"Are you going to sit there and play philosopher, or are you going to help me dig through all this valuable stuff," she demanded. When he failed to reply, she turned around to ask again.

The folding chair was empty.

Chapter 6

Steve arrived home shortly after six that evening, happy to see his wife's minivan parked in the garage. "I'm home!" he announced walking through the garage door into the kitchen. "Sandy?"

A trail of dirty clothes began just inside the master bedroom, sprinkled here and there on the way to the bathroom, which was still fogged over from the steam of a hot shower. He found her sound asleep on the living room couch. Her blonde hair soaking wet and an empty wine glass two feet away on the coffee table.

He leaned over, kissed her forehead, picked up the goblet, and retreated to the kitchen. Using his flip phone, he punched up Monical's Pizza. "I'd like to order a pizza for delivery please . . . Yes, a large pepperoni with extra onions, thin crust."

Steve's voice roused Sandy, who pulled herself up into a sitting position. "Steve?" When she realized what he was doing, she pulled herself to her feet and walked unsteadily halfway to the kitchen. "I'm so sorry, honey. I fell asleep," she mumbled. "I'll cook something."

Steve appeared around the corner and waved her off, pointing at his cell. "Ok, great, thirty minutes. Extra crispy. Perfect." She nodded drowsily, stumbled back to the living room, and dropped down onto the leather sofa with an exhausted moan.

"Are you kidding?" Steve said as he closed his phone and sat next to Sandy on the sofa. "I've been thinking about pizza all day. It'll be here in half an hour." He pulled his sleepy wife up by her shoulders and laid her head down in his lap. Like a limp doll, she acquiesced.

"How'd things go at the barn?" he asked, massaging her temples gently the way she liked.

"Even worse than I imagined," she replied, trying unsuccessfully to stifle a yawn. "I can't go back. My mom needs to sell the warehouse, as is, or I just might burn it down."

Steve stopped rubbing. "That bad?"

Sandy sat up and looked at him. "Steve—it's nothing but filth and garbage. The place is full of mold and mice poop. The lot it sits on is worth more without the building and everything in it."

"What can I do to help?" he asked.

"Nothing. You work all day—oh, and I found a dead raccoon behind one of the shelves. There are vines climbing up the inside back wall, a hole in the roof. A dozen wasp nests in the eaves—some of them are huge! It's disgusting."

"The place has its own eco-system." While Steve chuckled at his own joke, Sandy scrunched her eyebrows together as if trying to grasp why he would make light about what she was going through. "You'll get through it, love," he continued, adopting more empathetic tone. "Try to remember, you're not doing this for him but for your mom."

"Well, I found it completely embarrassing. I had a meltdown this morning and started screaming. I knocked over a pile of boxes, and they fell on top of me. Luckily, there was nothing but leaves in them."

"Leaves? As in tree leaves?" he asked.

"Yes. I couldn't believe it."

"Hmm. Okay," he continued. "But what was embarrassing about that?"

"Some guy poked his head in when I was having a fit because he thought I was being murdered or something. He rushed in to save me. I told him I'm not savable." She yawned. "I'm . . . in . . . Hell. And once you're there," she yawned a second time, "there's no escape."

"What guy?" asked Steve. When she didn't reply, he leaned over to find the love of his life fast asleep. Soft throaty whimpers came with each breath, the kind she made when she was utterly exhausted.

Steve kissed her eyelids, cradled her in his arms, and carried her to their bedroom. "Good night, love. You'll make it. One day at a time."

Chapter 7

The first thought to cross Sandy's mind the next morning when she realized she was awake was that she was in bed and had no idea how she had gotten there.

Bits and pieces of memory began forcing their way into her consciousness. Standing in the kitchen. Pouring wine. Laying on the sofa . . . Pizza . . . Leaves.

Leaves.

"Oh no," she moaned as she rolled onto her side. Her head throbbed. Every muscle in her body ached. She spotted the folded note on her nightstand taped to a bottle of Tylenol.

Good morning, Love.

I hope you don't mind that I didn't wake you. You needed your rest.
Take it day by day. Love always and forever.
— S

After throwing a couple tablets in her mouth and washing them down with a gulp of water from a glass Steve had left with his note,

Sandy walked into the bathroom and looked into the mirror. "Ugh," she groaned, turning away. She had considered skipping a shower, but her disheveled hair and stiff back convinced her otherwise.

Where would she find the strength to go back? While she was waiting for the water to get warm, she slammed down the toilet lid, sat down heavily, and sobbed.

Later that morning Sandy sat in her minivan studying the pole barn. How hard would it be to light it on fire? Would I die from smoke inhalation before the heat of the flames became unbearable? Would it be painful or over before I knew it?

Her thoughts wandered to her family and what life might be like for them without her. Her daughters were old enough to be okay with just Steve. He would be heartbroken, of course, but eventually he'd be okay, too. He was young enough and would remarry. Many single women in town would see him as a heck of a catch. Yes, her family would survive. She gripped the steering wheel tightly and closed her eyes.

Did anyone really need her any longer?

Today wasn't the first time she'd imagined this scenario. Death by fire was new, though. She used to imagine ending her life with a pill overdose, but changed her mind because an obvious suicide would be a terrible embarrassment not only to Steve, the girls, and her mom, but to her students and friends. But if this warehouse went up in flames, she thought, and she was trapped inside, it would seem like an accident. Tragic, of course, but an accident nonetheless.

Sandy took a deep breath, exhaled loudly, and shuttered at the dark thoughts consuming her. "My God, what I am thinking?" She started the minivan, slammed it into reverse, and backed out of the parking lot. It was already hot outside, and she needed something cold. Now.

The wall of cool air that greeted her when she opened the door and stepped into Berkelow's, the local grocery store, instantly refreshed her. What would the warehouse be like? "Hell," she muttered as she opened one of the cooler doors. "It'll be just like the hell it is."

"Excuse me?" asked an elderly lady standing just behind her. "Did you say something?"

"No, just singing a song," she said as she reached in and grabbed a bottle of diet peach Snapple. One of her former students, a red Berkelow's apron tied loosely over his street clothes, waited behind the checkout counter. Sandy put her tea on the check-out counter. "Hello, Paul."

"Hi, Mrs. Richards. Will that be all today?"

Instead of answering, Sandy stared blankly into space, clutching her purse tightly against her chest. An awkward silence lingered.

"Uh, Mrs. Richards? Did you forget something?"

"Oh, yes. Sorry Paul, I have a lot on my mind. I'll be right back."

Sandy walked away from the counter and down aisle 4, where she found another of her students busily stocking a shelf while humming a tune. He looked up and smiled when he saw her.

"Hey Mrs. Richards! How's your summer going?" asked Demetri with his own unique brand of enthusiasm. "Can I help you find something?"

"Hi, DT," she replied, calling him by his nickname. "That's quite a haircut," she said. Demetri had always been one of her favorites, and everyone knew it.

Demetri's face broke into a sheepish grin while he rubbed one of the nearly shaved sides of his head. "Yeah," he replied, brushing back the reddish brown mop on the top that had fallen over his forehead. "Things got out of hand the other night."

"I like it. It's you," she answered. "Do you . . ." She paused and stared down the aisle.

"Do I what, Mrs. Richards?" When she didn't answer, Demetri asked, "Are you okay? You look sort of pale."

"I'm fine," she shot back. "Just a lot on my mind. Do you have any matches?"

"I didn't know you smoked, Mrs. Richards."

"I don't—and you better not either!" She shook her index finger at her student. "Or chew."

"I don't," he replied, pointing down the aisle. "You'll find matches just around that end cap, on the left side."

Ten minutes later Sandy inserted the key into the corroded lock and pushed open the barn door. Hoping to catch a rare breeze, she left the door open when she walked inside. After a few seconds surveying the first tall stack dead ahead, she sighed loudly and shook her head. It was as if all her work the day before had never happened.

"You came back." The familiar voice was right behind her.

"That makes two of us," she replied, turning slowly around to face the stranger. He was dressed in what looked to be the same clothes he had on the day before: an olive-colored T-shirt, khaki pants, and shiny black boots.

"Good for you."

"Yeah," she responded sarcastically. "Good for me."

"My dad always said, 'You don't have to be the best, to be the best. You just have to be consistent.'" He laughed.

"Your dad?"

"Yes, my dad. He had a saying for every situation."

"I don't get it," she replied shaking her head. "You think I'm trying to be the best at something?"

"No, but you have a big job here," he said, casting his brown eyes from one end of the building to the other. "If you work consistently at this every day, you'll get it done. Right now, I suspect all this," he gestured with his right hand at the stacks of boxes, "is already beating you. Am I right?"

Sandy remained silent. Just who is this guy?

"I suspect you're not a quitter." Sam continued. "You're better than that. I believe you can beat this building, this mess." He looked deep into her eyes, so intensely Sandy felt she could not look away. "There are too many people in this world who simply give up. They walk away from their problems. Even worse, they become so overwhelmed they make the mistake of believing they just can't go on." He paused. "Do you know what I mean?"

"No, not really."

"What's in the bag?"

"A drink. Tea."

"The tea is in your hand," he said, nodding toward the bottle. "What's in the bag?"

When Sam eased closer, Sandy let the top of the bag fall open to reveal its contents. His eyebrows rose and he whistled through his teeth. "I wouldn't bring anything flammable into a place like this. What if you got trapped in here?" He walked in slow measured paces, looking back and forth as if seeing the inside of the barn for the first time. "A fire would spread quicker than lightning." He pointed toward the mountain of boxes lining the near side wall. "And because there are probably no chemicals in here in any quantity, well, smoke from wood, cardboard, and such would fill your lungs. But it wouldn't kill you. Not right away."

Sandy cocked her head as she listened, her mouth slowly falling open as she grasped the meaning of his words.

"The burning sensation, well that would be unbearable," Sam continued. "You might collapse near where the fire started." He looked around the floor and pointed. "Like there. Right there." She looked at the area he indicated and in her mind's eye saw her own body lying on the dirty floor.

"Smoke and heat like that incapacitates a person. You'd be unable to run from the flames, but you would be fully aware of what would be happening. The burning in your lungs and the lack of oxygen is paralyzing. But you would still be awake when the flames reach you."

Sandy gripped the plastic bag tightly and twisted it in her hands. "Stop, please," she whispered, looking straight down at the floor.

"You might even smell your burning flesh before you died. Your last moments of life would be indescribable in their agony."

Sandy lifted her eyes to look into his. "Why are you telling me this?"

Sam just smiled. "We should get those matches out of here." When she didn't reply, he added, "I think they're dangerous. What do you think?"

She slowly extended her hand holding the bag.

"Well, I don't want them!" he laughed. "Why don't you throw them in that dumpster I saw outside when I came in today?"

The burning in your lungs and the lack of oxygen is paralyzing. "Who are you?"

"I already told you. I'm Sam."

"Sam who?"

"Just Sam," he shrugged.

"Just Sam," she echoed, turning away from him to walk outside and toss the bag of matches into the brown metal dumpster Steve had rented and delivered early that morning. When she stepped back into the gloomy barn, it took a few moments for her eyes to adjust from bright sunshine to the shadowy interior.

"Sam?" She called out, walking deeper into the pole barn. "Sam?" The only voice she heard was her own bouncing off the rotting wooden walls. What the heck is with this guy?

Sandy took a large swig of her tea, grimaced because it was already warm, and began opening boxes.

Chapter 8

For Sandy and Tracey, Wednesday breakfasts were a summer break tradition. The morning interludes allowed the two friends to stay in touch and, in the right private setting, share professional ideas without having to worry about being overheard by other teachers or students. Their preferred out-of-the-way place to converse and catch up was their favorite booth in the Blue's Café at the corner of West Station Street and South Fraser Avenue in Kankakee. The local eatery was nothing much to look at from the outside, with its plain washed brown brick front, blue canvas awning, and red and blue sign crowned with a Pepsi bottle cap. But the food was always good, especially the homemade pies and the biscuits and gravy. And the service always came with a smile.

Anything you wanted to know about the events of the area could be learned by simply listening at Blue's. The morning gathering of local bankers, businessmen, and lawyers left nothing to the imagination. If it was happening in Kankakee County, they were discussing and dissecting it—loudly.

At Sandy and Tracey's table, the first fifteen minutes of conversation was dominated by Sandy, who described the interior of the old pole barn and the monumental size of the task her father had left to her. Tracey, of course, empathized and offered her help. They were midway through their bacon and eggs when Sandy got around to confessing that a stranger had been keeping her company in the barn. "I just might put him to work," she added. "You would think he would offer to help, right?"

"Whoa, what?" said Tracey, bursting out laughing. "Is he hot?" she asked, leaning forward to whisper the question.

"Tracey!" Sandy felt the blood rise in her cheeks and looked around the edge of their booth to make sure no one had heard.

"Come on. It's me—your partner in crime since grade school," Tracey prodded. "Besides, we're just a couple of old married women. Share." When Sandy met her gaze without replying, Tracey nodded. "Okay. Your silence says it all. He's hot. When can I meet your mysterious stranger?"

"He's not mine and he's not really a complete stranger anymore, Tracey." Sandy was sure by now her face was as red as her girlfriend's T-shirt.

"Look at you!" Tracey reached across the table and poked Sandy's forearm. "You are blushing! Do you like him?" She paused. "I'm living vicariously through you, girl. Describe him—and don't leave out a thing."

"No, I don't like him—not like that," shot back Sandy, who offered a slow shrug of the shoulders and tilted her head to the side. "He's hard to describe. Kind of tall, brownish hair—bad haircut."

"Bad haircut?"

"Well, not exactly a bad haircut. A chunk of hair is missing in the front, near where he parts it."

Tracey grimaced. "That's weird."

"Yeah, it is a little," admitted Sandy. "He is about six feet, well proportioned. That's about it, really."

"Don't give me that. You know what I really want to know," pressed Tracey, who smiled as she opened her mouth and filled it with a large bite of scrambled egg and toast.

Sandy used a forefinger to trace the wet circle her glass of orange juice had left on the table. "I'd say he's . . . attractive."

"So he's hot."

Sandy rolled her eyes. "Are we back in middle school?"

Tracey's head bobbed like a lovesick teenager. "Girl, we never left. We teach there, remember?" The observation triggered a mutual smile. Though neither said a word, each knew what the other was thinking.

Both were born to teach, but Sandy wanted to get away—far away. For years she had her sights set on California. Blue sky and sandy beaches were about as far away from Walton Center as she could get. Reality, however, intervened and the only job offer she received was at the school of their youth. Sandy reluctantly accepted, telling herself she would move west after one year. And then Tracey, who was hired by the same school a few weeks earlier, introduced Sandy to the new lawyer in town.

A Chicago boy, Steve Richards had been raised by a single mom in the Logan Square neighborhood on the north side in an apartment above the Terminal Restaurant. The young attorney with the Northwestern law degree thanked Tracey for the introduction, confiding to her after just two dates that Sandy Loucks was "the one." "I have always dreamed of running a successful one-man practice in a small Midwestern town," Steve explained, "meeting a local teacher, falling desperately in love, and raising a family." Tracey, of course, immediately shared all this with Sandy.

Their thoughts were interrupted when a waitress carrying two carafes of coffee, one regular and one decaf, stopped by the booth and asked, "Can I get you gals more coffee?"

Sandy was mixing half-and-half into her fresh cup when she leaned forward and whispered, "He came back yesterday."

"And?" Tracey stared at her, her own spoon hanging in midair.

"And what?" Sandy stared back.

"Fine," Tracey sighed with an exaggerated roll of the eyes. "Keep it a secret."

"I stopped by Berkelow's for a bottle of ice tea yesterday," began Sandy. She hesitated before continuing. "I bought some matches."

"Matches for what?" asked Tracey just before finishing her last bite of toast. "You don't smoke," she said between chews.

Sandy visibly stiffened. "It's not a crime to buy matches, is it?"

Tracey looked at her friend for several seconds. "No," she answered slowly. "But the last time I checked, arson was still a crime. Will they let us meet for breakfast on Wednesday mornings at Stateville?" She cut short her laugh when she saw the look on Sandy's face.

Her eyes were rimmed with dark circles, her brow furrowed in worry. Sandy lowered her voice another notch. "He asked me what I had in the bag. I told him—matches. It was like . . . like he knew."

The conversation had taken a sharp and sudden change in direction. "Shadow, talk to me."

"He went through this gruesome description of what it would be like to die in a fire. It was . . . awful. I could almost smell the smoke and feel the heat as he spoke."

Tracey reached out and laced the fingers of her right hand through Sandy's left. "Why did you buy those matches, Shadow?"

"Don't tell me you've never wondered."

"Wondered?" The pitch of Tracey's voice shot up an octave. "Are you saying what I think you are saying?"

"Shhhh," cautioned Sandy. "Keep your voice down!"

"Have I ever wondered what it would be like to burn down a building with me in it?" Her voice shook in a combination of anger and fear for her friend. "No, I can't say that I have."

Unable to look Tracey in the eye, Sandy stared down at her coffee cup. "Remember when we were in The Vanguard together, and we were competing at Geneseo for . . ."

Tracey squeezed her friend's hand and cut her off mid-sentence. "Don't change the subject. You know you can tell me anything."

"Alright," replied Sandy, lifting her eyes to meet Tracey's gaze. "I want options. That's all." Her usually soft and smooth voice had taken on an unexpected edgy and forceful tone. "I'm sick of not having options in my life. I stayed in Walton Center even though my dream was elsewhere. I have been teaching at the same school I attended for what, eighteen years? I stayed home to help my mom while my brothers were off to bigger things and brighter futures."

"But Shadow, you have a lovely family, a good career, and Steve," Tracey answered.

"What about Steve?" she shot back. "At least one of us got our dream. He has exactly what he always wanted—a successful small-town law practice, a nice little home, and a family and a wife. Why is it I'm always part of making everyone else's dreams come true while mine remain . . . dreams?" Sandy put her head into her hands and covered her eyes with her palms.

Tracey leaned back in the booth, her mouth open in dismay. "Shadow—where is this coming from?"

Instead of replying, Sandy lifted her head and stared out the café's plate glass window lost in thought.

Tracey leaned in again. "I'm not judging you, Shadow. Put yourself in my position," she pleaded, folding and unfolding a small paper napkin as she spoke. "My best friend just casually told me she's contemplating turning herself into a roasted marshmallow, and that she harbors a lot of resentment about the way her life is unfolding. Now she's surprised and withdrawn because I'm alarmed."

Sandy stood quickly, knocking a fork to the floor. "I have to run," she mumbled, digging in her purse for her wallet. "We'll talk soon." She glanced at the ticket, threw a five-dollar bill on the table, and walked away without another word.

"Wait! What? Shadow!" called out Tracey.

Tracey rested her elbows on the table and her chin between her cupped palms. Outside, her best friend climbed into her minivan and pulled away from the curb. Tracey bent down and picked up the fork. She had to help her friend, but she had no idea where to begin.

Chapter 9

Sandy was about to unlock the barn door when the sound of a loud engine caught her ear. It had been a long week, and the last thing she wanted or needed was a visitor.

She turned and watched as a bright blue, late-model Ford Mustang pulled into the parking lot. With the engine still running, a young man in his mid-20s stepped out and walked in her direction, slowing down to give the sprawling pole barn a good once-over. When he got within a few feet, Sandy realized he had a long blond ponytail running in front of his left ear halfway down his chest. The stranger flicked it behind him, smiled, lifted his sunglasses, and asked, "Are you Sandy Richards?"

"Yes," she said, taking a sip of water from a bottle of Crystal Springs. "Can I help you?"

He grinned and nodded. "You're the executor of Tom Loucks' estate, is that right?" Without waiting for a reply, he added, "So this is the place giving everyone such a fit. Heh."

Sandy's eyes narrowed. "Yes, I'm his daughter. And what fit are you talking about?"

"Never mind," he replied, reaching inside his light jacket to withdraw an envelope. He handed it to her and she took it. "Consider yourself served, Mrs. Richards."

"Served? What!" shrieked Sandy, her eyes darting back and forth between the envelope and the ponytailed man. "What is this about? Served with what?"

"I'm sorry," he shrugged, looking like he actually meant it. "It's just a job, lady. I gotta save for college."

With that, the process server trotted back to his car and climbed in. Sandy chased after him, waving the envelope in one hand while crying for him to stop. The muscle car fishtailed out of the parking lot well ahead of her with a heavy metal tune blaring out of the open windows.

Sandy turned the envelope over and read the front. It was addressed to her parents. Her eyes slowly moved up and left to settle on the sender:

Property Tax Division
Illinois Department of Revenue
PO Box 19033
Springfield, IL 62794-9033

She let out a groan and, with deliberation the school's biology teacher would have appreciated, carefully opened the letter along the top. Sandy's hand shot to her mouth to stifle a cry.

Re: 30-Day Notice to Auction Sale

Dear Tom and Dorothy Loucks

A lien has been filed against the property listed above for unpaid taxes for the years 1992-1994, and for tax returns that have not been filed or were not filed properly. Penalty assessments have also been issued, and a judgment against you was entered by the Attorney General.

Her dad had been ignoring tax notifications and not filing his returns? She began pacing up and down the edge of the driveway and continued reading:

Collection Action We May Take: Seizure

We are authorized by law to attempt to collect the debt. Therefore, on July 10, 1995 at 9:00 a.m., your property will be put up for auction and the proceeds utilized to . . .

The letter and envelope fluttered as one to the ground. "No. No. No!" she said over and over, walking in small tight circles through knee-high grass bordering the parking lot. A wave of nausea swept over her and she fell to her hands and knees, vomiting what was left of the eggs, bacon, and toast she had eaten with Tracey at the Blues Café.

And then she wept.

The water in the bottle was warm, but she used it to wash the bitter taste from her mouth. She pulled out her phone and called Steve, but the message went to voicemail. Only then did she recall he was in trial all day and unavailable.

Sandy sat in the grass for a full fifteen minutes staring at the letter beside her. Two weeks. She had only fourteen days to sort through this old barn before it and everything in it would be sold to some stranger.

She picked up the letter and envelope and walked unsteadily back to the door. She was about to insert the key when the door eased open on its own with the lightest of touch.

"You're late." A figure stepped out of the darkness into the broad beam of sunlight streaming through the front entrance.

A wave of irritation rose inside her. "How'd you get in here?"

"Good morning to you, too," he teased. "You should be more careful. The door was unlocked. I arrived a couple minutes ago thinking you were already here."

"Look, why do you keep coming back? You know I have work to do." Her mind went back to Tracey's comments an hour earlier in the Blue's Café. "And that I'm married."

Sam's eyes opened wide at the last comment "Oh I am fully aware of that—the married part. After yesterday, well, I thought I would check in on you." His eyes took in the vomit stains on her t-shirt, the red rings around her eyes, and the letter in her hand. "You seem in need of a friend. What's wrong?"

"You don't know me. How can you possibly know what I need?"

"Well, life's a mystery, that's for sure. But you've been crying, and I have a suspicion that letter has something to do with it."

Sandy silently handed him the envelope, which he opened as he moved a few steps back and sat down in the same folding chair against the front wall. "Hmm," he said several times as he read through the legalese. "Hmm." When he finished he looked up at her, his eyes filled with visible pain. "I can see why you were crying now. This puts a lot of stress on you and your mom."

"Yup," Sandy began. "Life is hard. We all make choices and we have to live with the consequences—even when your dad doesn't bother to pay his taxes. You know," she added, "I bet they might come and take my mom's small house, too."

"Maybe your husband can do something," he suggested. "He's an attorney, right?"

She nodded and her thoughts fell back to her earlier conversation with Tracey. "Where do you live?"

Sam tilted his head toward the door. "Around the corner."

"The old dam in the river is around the corner. When you turn the corner, you cross the bridge," she shot back. Sam didn't answer. "Are you a troll living under the bridge?" she asked in a mocking tone.

"Nope. Not a troll." He looked up and slowly turned his head to take in the mounds of boxes, bags, and other items stacked high around them. "In truth, Sandy," Sam said standing up, "I came back today to help you."

"Well, that would be a change," she replied. She immediately regretted the sharp tone in her voice. "I need help," she began again, softening her voice. "I would appreciate any you can give me."

"It may not be exactly the kind of help you expect."

"I'll take whatever help I can get," she replied before turning back to her work.

Sandy crab-walked backward, dragging a half-dozen crushed cardboard containers to the front of the barn to throw away that evening. She dropped the load where it belonged, straightened at the waist with a groan, and clapped her canvas-gloved hands together. Puffs of dust exploded into the hot air that hung heavy and still inside the old pole barn.

Sam smiled. "You seem to get quite a kick out of that."

Sandy sat down with a sigh onto the stack of cardboard. "Leaves and more leaves. What a surprise." She shook her head slowly. "Today I have found several boxes of moldy old clothes I would be too embarrassed to offer to the Salvation Army, more boxes filled with newspapers, magazines, and other junk—all of which looked like it was soaked before it was boxed," she continued, "and of course, leaves." She coughed a couple times to clear her throat. "I stopped counting the plastic bags full of them." She took a long drink from her bottle of lukewarm diet tea, wiped her chin, and studied Sam. "Do you actually do anything?" she asked.

"I'm here to help," he replied.

"Works for me." Sandy stood and pulled down another box. When she opened it and found nothing inside but more leaves, she stifled a scream and shoved the cardboard container behind her.

After fifteen minutes of silence broken only by a few grunts of effort and groans of dissatisfaction, Sam broke their silence. "Your intensity amazes me. Tell me about yourself."

"About me?" she replied looking up. "Only if you promise to begin working instead of just talking about it. And," she added with a grunt when she shoved a large box ahead of her, "this is going to be a boring conversation."

"I suspect not." Sam leaned forward and rested his elbows on a stack of boxes, his chin on his hands.

"I'm a wife, mother, and teacher. Not much more to tell."

"You've told me *what* you do. Now tell me *who* you are."

Sandy was opening a large black bag when she stopped and cocked her head to look at him. "No one has ever asked me that. I'm not sure I know."

"What grade and what do you teach?"

"Four through twelve. Instrumental music. I spend most of my day at the middle school, but I also start beginners in the lower grades and teach high school band. It's a small district with a small budget. All three schools are on one small campus, so I can do it all."

"Why music?"

"Why don't you ask me why I breathe?"

By this time Sam had settled back into the folding chair. Sandy eased her way a few feet closer. She took in the slits of sunlight filtering through the water-stained ceiling, and noticed for the first time the various shades of color pouring in. Her face beamed. "I live to teach. It's a calling. I'd do it for free if I had to," she began. "There is nothing quite like placing a musical instrument in the hands of a fourth grader for the first time, and helping them learn the joys of music. The wonderment in their eyes when what they play after hard work morphs into recognizable music is amazing." Standing, she brushed dust from the back of her jeans and continued, too excited to sit still. "The final time our band plays every year is at high school graduation. The seniors, wearing robes, leave their seats to join the band for one last musical performance. Knowing I've played a big role in bringing music into their lives and their hearts, Sam, well . . . it's a joy of indescribable intensity. After graduation, some will never play again. Others will continue into college and beyond." She paused and looked directly at him. "A few will make it their life's work through teaching or performing."

"Tell me more about them, the ones who stick with it." His voice made it clear he was genuinely interested in what was important to her.

"Have you ever heard of the rock band Arminius?" she asked. Sam shook his head. "Robbie Craft is Arminius's drummer. I taught him how to hold his sticks. Then there's Candace Stewart. She's now the music teacher at Mark Twain Grade School in Kankakee."

"And does Candace bring the same level of enthusiasm and joy to her students?" he asked.

"Absolutely," beamed Sandy. "She's a special young woman. She attended VanderCook College of Music in Chicago after graduating from Walton Center."

"Where did you go to college?"

"VanderCook."

"So she was inspired by you. She wanted to be just like... you."

"I don't know," replied Sandy, who could feel her cheeks turning red. "She loves teaching as much as I do. I remember the day I taught her how to hold her trumpet and form her lips." Her excitement was palpable. "I have a couple of former students on full music college scholarships. I have no idea how many others are in college playing music. I can't keep track of them all. Some stay in touch, others don't. Sometimes I run into their parents and they tell me how there kids are doing. I love hearing about them."

A wide toothy smile broke out across Sam's face. "I can hear it in your voice."

"There's an amazing young man named Chris Hill. He played trombone but loved the guitar. He's a praise and worship leader at Olivet Nazarene University. I'm not sure what a praise and worship leader is, exactly," she chuckled, "but I hear the students at ONU love him. It may be a cliché, but music is indeed the universal language."

"Life is enriched through music."

"Reading and playing music is like reading and speaking another language," continued Sandy. "Playing an instrument enhances creativity, advances problem-solving skills, and raises IQ. It's true. I see it all the time. Music is math. Music is science. It's art. It's history. Music is a complete language. And if you're in a competitive marching band, or in drum and bugle corps, it can also be a sport. Drum Corps International is marching music's major league."

"The look of true accomplishment is marching across your face," he replied.

"Is it?" she asked touching her cheeks with both palms. "Yes, it probably is." She made no attempt to stifle a grin brought about through a fond recollection. "In 1972 I marched and competed with the Des Plaines Vanguard Drum and Bugle Corps in the first ever Drum Corps International Championship. I'll cherish the experience for the rest of my life."

"I wish someone had put an instrument into my hands."

"I was going to ask you if you played," she replied. "My students probably don't remember the first moment I placed an instrument in their little hands and showed them how to hold it and make a sound."

"Do you remember the first time you held an instrument?" he asked.

She nodded with renewed energy. "I was in fourth grade. My father drove me to Agatone's Music Store in Kankakee. I still remember standing at the glass counter. My father was talking to a man with a heavy accent. I later learned he was Italian. Mr. Agatone placed a little black case on top of the glass counter. My first clarinet was in that case." She paused, her eyes screwed shut drawing forth a memory long since buried. "I remember my dad picking up the instrument and handing it to me." She looked at her filthy hands as if she expected her first clarinet to miraculously appear. "Sam, that magical moment changed my life forever." The thought brought tears welling up in her eyes. She turned aside and quickly brushed them away hoping Sam didn't notice.

"Those are wonderful memories, Sandy," he replied. "Just thinking about your dad giving you that clarinet transformed your face. You're absolutely radiant."

She ignored his comment and rattled on. "I played clarinet all through grade school. It wasn't much of a challenge, so Mr.

Higgerson, my music teacher, switched me to the oboe. It was love at first squeak!" Both of them laughed together.

"What do you remember about your first oboe?" he inquired.

"I recall my father coming home from work at the steel mill. He told me he forgot something in the back seat. 'Shadow,' he said—that's what he called me, Shadow—'can you go get it?' And there it was, a black glistening oboe trimmed with silver, nestled there in an open case lined with blue." Still smiling, she continued, "I still have that beautiful little instrument."

"You still have it? That says a lot about you," nodded Sam. "I bet your students love you."

"I hope they do. It's completely mutual. Teaching kids to make music is my passion."

"They would miss you if you left."

She shrugged. "A few, maybe. Some more than others." She shrugged. "But a new music teacher would take my place. Life goes on. I think they love the music, not me."

"Sure life goes on, but my guess is they want to emulate you. Powerful stuff, emulation and respect. You're a positive example."

Sandy shrugged, turned, and wiped away another tear—but not before it had run halfway down her right cheek.

The sound of a falling box echoed through the building. Sandy moved quickly around the tall pile to find a long cardboard container. The rotten tape holding it together had ripped open. A pile of leaves had spilled out onto the dirty floor. She spent a few seconds pushing them back into the box and walked back with it to the front of the barn. The chair was folded and leaned back up against the wall. Sam was no where to be seen.

"Oh, for heaven's sake. Where has that confusing man gone now?"

Chapter 10

Hands in the air, Sandy was standing in her mom's small kitchen waving the envelope from the Illinois Department of Revenue as if fanning a fire. Even the smell of her favorite breakfast simmering in a skillet could not calm her down. "And you did what?"

Dorothy left the stove and sat down at the table, folding her hands in her lap after wiping them on her apron. She avoided her daughter's angry stare. In front of her was a similar tax lien notice, this one against the house. She finally mustered the strength to speak. "Please don't use that tone with me." She sounded like she wanted to cry. "You father took the papers we got in the mail and said he had it under control."

"But he had nothing under control!" Sandy retorted, her face red with anger. "Mom, what were you thinking?"

"Your father handled all the finances. I . . . I didn't know he wasn't paying the taxes."

"For a few years he didn't even file taxes, mom!" Sandy picked up the notice off the table with her free hand, shook her head, and threw it back down. "How could you stay married to him?" she demanded. "How could you let him blow through everything and leave you bankrupt?"

Someone on the back porch cleared a throat and pushed open the screen door. The women turned to spot Tracey standing in the kitchen, a wide if wholly fake smile glued to her face. "Hi Sandy, Mrs. Loucks." She focused her attention on Sandy. "Instead of breakfast, how about we take a walk, girlfriend?"

The girls had accepted Dorothy's breakfast invitation that Wednesday morning instead of making their usual pilgrimage to Blue's Cafe. In her anger, Sandy had forgotten all about it.

"Not now, Tracey, I—" Sandy began.

Tracey cut her off. "Your mom needs some time alone, Sandy." She held the door open. Sandy nodded, shot a look at her mom, and stomped outside.

With a gentle hand on her friend's elbow, Tracey guided them down steps, around the house, and out to the sidewalk.

"That was uncalled for," she began, keeping her eyes glued ahead as they took up a slow pace down the block. Sandy remained silent. "Your mom has no blame here and she is not the real target of your anger. Which means," continued Tracey, "we are back to your dad. So tell me again where all this anger is coming from."

Sandy stopped walking and turned to face Tracey. "You, of all people, should understand."

Tracey tugged on her arm and the walk resumed. "Well I guess I don't. So maybe it is best to just vomit all that poison right now."

Sandy shrugged. "Why?"

"Because I'm worried about you. This pent up anger you're carrying around is tearing you apart, and if you haven't noticed," she added, gripping Sandy's arm a bit tighter, "it's hurting your relationships in every direction—your husband, your girls, and now your dear old mom. And God knows it's wearing on me," she admitted. "So let's get it out. I know you loved your father . . ."

"I thought the sun rose and set on his command," blurted out Sandy. "I would've done anything for him. But he changed."

"We all change, Shadow. Life changes us."

"Not like he changed."

Tracey chose her words carefully. "Judging other people can be . . . dangerous. No one is perfect and we have all made mistakes large and small." Sandy remained silent. Tracey continued. "Your kids are watching and listening. You are teaching them that it is normal and acceptable to be this angry over past transgressions, girl. Fast forward fifteen years. Emiley and Sarah will be judging you harshly like you are judging your dad."

"That's ridiculous," spat Sandy. Now it was Tracey's turn to remain silent. "That will never happen to me."

"Years from now, Em and Sarah may be mad at you over something in the past, some mistake or bad decision or some low point in your life and overlook all the good you did," continued Tracey. "Your relationship with your kids will be destroyed because they've seen your example. This is a very unhealthy thing you're engaged in."

"My relationship with them is solid." Sandy dismissed the entire idea with a wave of her hand. "I'm nothing like Tom Loucks. Thank you very much."

Tracey stopped and turned to face her best friend, this time with one hand on each of Sandy's arms. "You need to get a grip on this escalating anger! Your dad gave you life! He gave you years of happiness and a home and food and shelter. And then he fell down and it hurt everyone." She paused, looking into a stone cold gaze. "Don't you think if he could do it all over he would do it differently?"

Sandy rolled her shoulders to throw off Tracey's hands. "Maybe our breakfast get-togethers aren't what's healthy," she shot back. "For some reason, they're turning into 'Let's get together and pick on Sandy' sessions. I don't need this." Sandy turned around and started walking back toward her mother's house.

"You still haven't told me why."

Sandy walked a few more steps before stopping. "Why what?" she asked without turning around.

"Why you have so much hate for your dad."

Sandy's legs felt suddenly weak, and with a long slow sigh she sat down right there on the sideway. Tracey walked over and sat beside her.

"When he worked at the steel mill," began Sandy, "he was a normal, almost Father Knows Best kind of dad. We did everything together. He read to me, taught me how to write, tucked me in every night with a story." She stopped and looked away, quickly brushing away a tear before continuing. "Then he went back to school. He became obsessed with education. Got a bachelor's degree, then started his MBA. We didn't…"

"Shadow," Tracey broke in gently. "Maybe try using I instead of we. Speak only for yourself. I'm not sure your family shares your view of your father."

Sandy tilted her head to one side and furrowed her brow while considering the suggestion. "I didn't see him much when I was twelve, thirteen," she continued. "When I did, he had his nose stuck in a book. Maybe it's not fair, but before that, it seemed like I was the only person who existed to him. When I turned twelve, it was like he forgot who I was."

"He was busy doing adult things, Shadow. We all get busy. Providing for a family in that generation when moms stayed home—that put a lot of pressure on the bread winner."

Sandy shrugged lightly and continued. "He got his Masters and quit his job at the mill. That's when our lives began to turn upside down."

"How so?" asked Tracey.

"First, it was 'no-money-down real estate.' He was going to make a million buying homes of little value, for nothing down and one hundred percent financing." Sandy grimaced. "He bought two old deteriorating houses to start and made our entire family scrub floors, paint, and pull weeds to clean them up. When the recession hit, he lost one back to the bank and sold the other at a loss."

"Entrepreneurs take risks," offered Tracey.

"This particular entrepreneur risked his whole family," replied Sandy. "Then he bought that little candy shop in Chicago Heights. He hired a manager and left him without supervision. Of course the man robbed my dad blind. He walked away from the candy business," she continued, "and bought the diner and had us all washing dishes, cooking, and cleaning tables. None of us signed up for that!" she added, the anger in her voice rising. "We rolled with his every whim. We had no say in the matter. Then," Sandy's tone took on a bitter edge, "the drinking began. Sure, he drank some all along, but now he was really throwing them back."

Sandy paused, reaching down to pluck a dandelion out from between the cracks of the cement. "One morning before school I was washing dishes at the diner and heard a woman scream. I ran out of the kitchen just in time to see my dad punch a young customer. I was scared to death. The boy ran out the door holding his bloody nose."

Her words came faster now as the story picked up steam. "Thank God my father didn't chase him. But keep in mind, it was around six-thirty in the morning. I saw my father pull out a bottle of bourbon from under the sink and take a long swig. He looked right at me." Tears welled in her eyes and spilled over onto her cheeks. "He swore and screamed at me to get out. I cried all the way home, his words echoing in my head: 'Get out! Get out! Get out!' I never worked another day in that greasy spoon."

"I remember now," whispered Tracey. "The family sued, right?"

Sandy nodded. "He was only fifteen. They settled out of court. I don't know for how much." She used her sleeve to wipe her runny nose. "Guess why my father hit him."

"I have no idea."

"Because he had a German accent."

"Really?" Tracey's head fell back slightly and her mouth fell open. "That might explain why he went ballistic years later when you bought that Volkswagen."

"Exactly!" She brushed back her hair with one hand. "Later when I was in college and home for spring break, my dad asked me one night at the dinner table what I thought about the war in Vietnam. I was so happy he wanted my opinion and I foolishly took it as a sign that he finally respected me as an adult." She sighed as she shook her head. "I gave him the standard college student answer for everything, 'Make love, not war.' And then his onslaught began."

"How so?"

"He stood up and yelled, 'You don't know what you're talking about. Stand for something or you'll fall for anything. Communism has to be stopped.' Blah, blah, blah.' And then, the oddest thing happened." Sandy stopped to study a thumb nail, which she nibbled on for a few seconds. "He began to sob. I'd never seen him cry. Through his sobbing, he screamed that I had no idea what war was like. He said to take the life of another human being was the worst thing a person could do, but sometimes it had to be done. He knocked the chair over as he left the house. I can still hear the sound of his tires squealing down the street."

"I had no idea, Shadow," Tracey said slowly. "You've never told me any of this."

"Dirty laundry and all. My mom always taught us to keep family matters in the family. Mostly that makes sense, I guess. Anyway, he didn't come home. Mom slept on the sofa that night. The police brought him home about two in the morning, dead drunk. He had passed out in his car behind the American Legion."

"So this was like, twenty years ago?" asked Tracey.

Sandy nodded. "Things only got worse from there. He could never watch a war movie, but now he would just look at one and start crying. Last year, it all came crashing down when the County Health Department shut down his restaurant."

"That I remember," admitted Tracey. "The headline on Chicago News 9 was 'Seventy-year-old World War II vet arrested for attacking a Walton Center health code enforcement officer.'"

"The outpouring of support that flooded in from all over the country only encouraged him," continued Sandy. "When we tried to bail him out of jail, he refused to leave. He just kept screaming at the police about how he had been saving the free world from the Nazis before the cops were born. He babbled on and on, something about how he had become a political prisoner of the country he'd fought to save."

"How embarrassing that must have been."

"My poor mom."

"Shadow, what did your dad do during the war?"

"How would I know?" Sandy said, leaning back as if she had been lightly pushed. "He never talked about it unless he was spouting some angry lecture. If I've heard it once, I've heard it a hundred times. 'You have no idea what war is like. It's not like the stupid movies.'" Her eyes narrowed. "Now can we please change the subject? I am exhausted."

Tracey offered a vigorous nod. "Sure. That's about all the Family Feud I can take for one day." Tracey's face lit up. "Hey, I'm off from my summer job tomorrow. Can I come down and help you with the great pole barn summer cleanup?"

"Seriously? That would be wonderful!" exclaimed Sandy as she leaned forward to hug her friend.

"As a heart attack. Will Mr. Handsomely Mysterious be there?"

"I don't keep his schedule, dear, but he hasn't missed a day yet. In fact, if I'm late, he's usually there waiting for me. In a strange way, he's sorta' holding me accountable."

"Think he'll hold me?" A smile spread across Tracey's face.

"Accountable. I'm talking accountable here."

Sandy stood up, reached down, and pulled Tracey to her feet. "Let's head back. I have an apology to deliver."

Chapter 11

The pending tax auction, coupled with her promise to her mother to clean the barn, added a new-found sense of urgency to Sandy's efforts. The first few weeks of summer vacation flew by, fueled by a relentless schedule from which she rarely deviated.

Sandy was up shortly after dawn, made sure the girls were set with their activities, and rarely opened the door to the barn later than 8:00 a.m. The routine was grueling, but the structure helped her stay on course. The junk—stacked high in thick identifiable fingers pointing toward the rafters—helped her determine exactly how many she had to go through each day to stay on schedule. She opened every container of every size and shape, decided what if anything was worth keeping, and dumped the rest in the trash bin outside the door. There was so much to go through that Steve ordered up two more bins, and all three (plus the ground surrounding them) were filled to capacity by the time she left each evening just before dinner time. She had gone through nearly two dozen stacks, and almost nothing had been worth saving.

And on each day, except two, Sam paid her a visit. On those days when he stayed but a few minutes, he would tell her, "I have a lot to do, and just wanted to check in on you." On others he would pitch in and offer to help, but he talked a lot more than he worked, if he worked at all. When he didn't appear one Monday morning, Sandy grew concerned. By the time afternoon rolled around, a certain sadness mixed with a fresh sense of hurt engulfed her. She barely slept that night, wondering whether he would ever show up again.

The next morning, when he popped his head around a heap of empty boxes with a smile and a cheery hello, she ignored him for a handful of seconds before relenting enough to put her hands on her hips, blow loose strands of hair away from her face, and demand, "Where were you yesterday?"

"I was busy," he replied, a faint grin still tracing his face. "Did you miss me?"

"No," she gasped, bending down to pick up a dirty box. "Too busy to help me?" she asked, tossing the filthy container in his direction.

Sam caught it without blinking an eye. "Even when I am not here, I am helping you."

Sandy threw back the corner of a black canvas tarp to reveal an old dresser. A hard pull of the handle convinced the warped top drawer to give way against its will to reveal nothing but mice droppings and old nests made of bits of leaves and grass. "How do you figure?" she shot back, searching the next two drawers with the same empty results.

"You were thinking of me, right?" Sam answered. "Positive thoughts."

Sandy caught the twinkle in his brown eyes. "Darn it, Tracey," she thought. "Why do you have me thinking like this?"

Chapter 12

Sandy laughed when she pulled up next to Tracey's vehicle at the pole barn the next morning. Her friend was still behind the wheel but dancing in her seat, mouthing the words to a muffled song blaring on her radio. When Tracey caught sight of Sandy climbing out of her van, she opened her car door to let "Not Fade Away" spill out into the morning stillness.

"Oh please turn it off!" laughed Sandy. "That old music dates us! Can't you find something more current?"

"Are you kidding me?" shot back Tracey while she continued bobbing and weaving in her seat. "Buddy Holly is ageless and that song is a classic!"

"Haven't you heard the stuff they're playing today on 99.9? Don't you listen to The Bus?" She was referring to WBUS, Kankakee's Top Forty station. "'It's a double-decker weekend on The Bus,'" she drolled in in her best Top 40 radio announcer voice.

Tracey laughed. "At least I'm not listening to the Macarena. That dance is too hard to do behind a steering wheel." Flipping off the radio, she got out of her car. "Speaking of our oldie moldy past, our glory days wearing the red and black, look what I have!" She fanned out four event tickets like an expert card dealer in Vegas.

"What are they?" asked Sandy.

"You've been working your summer away like a champ, so I decided we all need a break. I bought tickets to Drum Corps Midwest Championships. It's next Saturday at Huskie Stadium in Dekalb."

"Four?" The excitement spread across her face as she took the tickets from Tracey. "Who else do we know who is silly enough to want to spend a Saturday night watching Drum Corps Midwest Championships?"

Tracey turned her palms up in surprise. "Hmm. That would be our husbands for four hundred, Alex!"

Sandy rolled her eyes heavenward. "Steve says watching a drum corps is like watching grass grow. He'll never go. Even if he did, he'd make sure we all felt his misery."

"That's his problem. He should be watching the drum corps, not staring at the grass on the field," laughed Tracey. "Wait . . . Huskie Stadium is artificial turf. If he's waiting for that to grow, he has a different set of problems."

"Right. I'm certain that'll solve everything."

"I already asked him," she grinned. "He can't wait!"

"You asked Steve and he agreed?" Sandy's face made it clear she didn't believe her.

"He surely did."

"Well, we'll see," Sandy answered. "But I'm telling you, he'll make us miserable with constant observations. Here's his favorite: 'A football field is for football and a concert hall is for music.'"

"We're going and so is Steve." Tracey turned to face the barn. "Let's get to work. Wait," she said, looking around as if searching for something. "So?"

"So, what?"

"So where is he?"

"I told you. He just shows up when I least expect it. His attendance is better than our students' attendance."

"Well, let's dig into those stacks," she said walking toward the door with Sandy trotting behind her to catch up. "Maybe he won't show if he thinks we're waiting for him, Shadow. So, let's pretend we don't care if he shows or not and maybe he will."

Sandy pulled up the key on her ring and inserted it into the door. "We don't care."

"Sure," Tracey nudged her in the side with her elbow. "Speak for yourself. I want to meet this guy. I make light of it, but I think you're a bit emotionally challenged right now. I'd really love to know this guy's intentions."

The key clicked in the lock and the door creaked open. "It's not like that," Sandy replied, as she was about to step inside the barn. "Are you coming?"

A more serious look passed across Tracey's face. "Let's think like adults here. Pretend it was your daughter working in this barn and some stranger kept hanging around. Wouldn't you wonder about his intentions?"

"Tracey, I appreciate your concern. I really do. But I am an adult, and there's nothing going on here other than cleaning." She glanced coyly at her friend. "And friendship, maybe."

"That's what I mean," continued Tracey. "I don't think a man and woman can have a growing friendship and be alone in a deserted barn day after day and not be headed toward disaster. Especially a woman who is struggling with her emotions."

Sandy ignored her friend's admonition and disappeared inside. Tracey followed a few feet behind her, looking up and down at the piled of trash and junk.

"You've really been working for weeks here?"

Sandy looked crestfallen. "Can't you tell?"

"I didn't see it in the beginning," backpedaled Tracey. "I guess I'm just . . . shocked . . . at how much still has to be done. I'm sorry I haven't been much help. What can I do?"

Sandy explained what she needed done, and Tracy disappeared around a giant mount of blue and black garbage bags to begin work.

"I'm a-gonna tell you how it's gonna be," sang Tracey. "You're gonna give your love to me."

"You're a choral teacher, Tracey—no singing unless you are on key," laughed Sandy. She turned around to get her box knife and nearly cried out in surprise. A smiling Sam was just a few feet behind her. He raised his right index finger to his lip.

"Don't introduce me," he whispered.

"Why?" she whispered back.

"Why haven't I been here yet to help?" shouted Tracey from behind her wall of bags. "I have to work a summer job, you know! One of us doesn't have a lawyer for a husband. We're common hardworking country folk. That's why not."

"I wasn't aware you had a guest," Sam whispered. "She won't understand."

"I don't understand, Sam," Sandy whispered, her back still to Tracey.

"Sandy, please stop. This won't go well for you," he responded as he slowly backed up.

"I don't understand anything about this Sam guy. I'm telling you, he wants something." Tracey stepped around the bags with her hands on her hips.

Sandy turned to face her glare. She hadn't seen him? "Tracey," she said, grabbing her shoulders in an effort to spin her around. "Quick, look over by the door."

Tracey turned toward the battered entrance. "Why?"

Sandy turned and looked, but Sam was gone.

Chapter 13

Steve ran out of the office building, hopped into his red Ford-150 truck, revved the engine several times, and then headed for the pole barn. With the sound of Three Dog Night blaring from his radio, he tapped the steering wheel with his gold wedding ring, slowed for a red light, tilted his head back, and howled as long and loud as he could. When he stopped, he looked out his open window and spotted an older woman in a plain skirt and brown blouse who had stopped to stare at him and shake her head from the sidewalk not twenty feet away.

"Mrs. Watson!" he shouted, slapping the steering wheel with both hands. He had just finished drafting her will and setting up her trust the week before. "Eli's coming! Every girl in town had better hide her heart!" Mrs. Watson cocked her head and watched him drive off, looking as though she had just seen a spaceship land on main street.

Two minutes later Steve was running inside the barn door. "Sandy!" he yelled. "Love? Where are you?"

"Steve? I'm back here!" came the muffled voice of his wife, who appeared in body fifty feet away dripping sweat from her face while wiping her hands on the front of her filthy denim jeans.

"You'll never guess what's happened!" he exclaimed as he picked her up and spun his wife around in his arms.

"What in the world has gotten into you Steve Richards?" she giggled. "Put me down."

"Not until you guess," he teased. "Eli's coming."

"Steve, have you lost your mind? Eli who?"

"Better hide your heart, girl!" He spun her a second time. Halfway around Sandy caught a glimpse of Sam standing in a narrow lane between two mountains of refuse. When had he come in?

"Channeling your inner Three Dog Night, are you?" she asked. "So what's up with you and Tracey these days?" Steve stopped spinning and gave his wife a puzzled look. "Never mind. I'll tell you later," continued Sandy. "And why are you so happy?" She strained her neck, but Sam was no longer there. "And put me down please."

"I'll tell you why, woman. But I am not putting you down until I do." He hoisted her up a bit to change position, leaned in until his nose touched hers, and announced, "I just got out of binding arbitration. He awarded us just north of a million bucks!"

Sandy's eyes widened as she wiggled an arm free to cover her open mouth. "The guy over in Joilet in a wheel chair for life because of a drunk driver? I forgot that was today!"

"That's the one!" Steve said as he lowered her to the ground. "It's one of the largest awards in years in this stingy defense-oriented county, too!" He glanced at his watch. "I have to get back to the office and write up a few things and make some calls," he continued, nearly out of breath from the excitement. He gave her a quick kiss, turned and called over his shoulder. "See you tonight. I love you!"

"Wait!" exclaimed Sandy with both her hands palm-out in front of her like a pair of stop signs. "I want to introduce you to . . ." She turned to look but Sam was gone. She trotted back to where he had been standing, but the aisle she was sure he had slipped into was empty.

"What?" asked Steve, standing in the doorway.

"Nothing," she said shaking her head. "I'll be home in time to get dinner on the table."

"Don't worry—I'll pick up a couple of Aurelio's pizzas so we can relax and enjoy the evening."

Once Steve was gone, Sandy crossed her arms and screwed up her face into a deep grimace. "Sam?" No reply. "You did not go out that door, so you are here somewhere. I know it."

"He loves you." She heard his voice before she saw him. *He loves you.* The words echoed in her head and seemed to be coming from every direction.

He. Loves. You.

After wasting several minutes trying to locate him in amid the mountains of trash, she found him in the usual place—sitting on his folding chair twenty feet from the door.

She folded her arms across her chest and sucked in a deep breath. "This is not funny."

"It wasn't meant to be," replied Sam. "He really does love you."

"Yes, I know he loves me," she admitted. "He's never rude, but he didn't even say hello. I'm embarrassed."

"He didn't see me," answered Sam.

"He was spinning me around, Sam. If I saw you, so did he."

"No, you were in front of his eyes, and he only had eyes for you," he said in nearly a whisper. "He made time to drive over and share his good news with you. That is not always common in couples, you know. He loves you."

"Why do you keep saying that?" she asked. "We're married. We have kids. I certainly hope he loves me!"

Sam walked next to Sandy toward the front of the barn. "Lots of men who have kids never love the woman to begin with. Either that, or they fall out of love, or vice versa. But not him. You can see it in his eyes . . . the way he holds and looks at you. His enthusiasm in sharing his joy with only one person. You. This man adores you."

"Relationships can be fragile alliances." She softened her tone. "We are having a tough time right now." Sandy watched Sam acknowledge that fact with a knowing nod of his head. "Are you married, Sam?"

"I was. It was a long time ago."

"You're not very old," she replied. "It couldn't have been that long ago. Does she live around here?"

"She died of cancer."

"Oh my gosh, she must have been so young. I'm sorry, Sam."

"Me too, and thank you. She's in a better place." His voice was calm, steady.

"That's what they say."

"You don't believe in an afterlife?" he asked.

"I don't know," began Sandy. "I go to church, well, now and then. Every once in a while, I guess." His stare made her uncomfortable and she shifted her weight from one foot to the other. "Easter—two years ago. Maybe three."

"So it's been a while."

"Are you judging me?"

"Nope."

Sandy shrugged. "I get it. Noah built an ark. Joshua's trumpets blew the walls down. Jonah was swallowed by a whale and lived to tell about it. Oh yes, and Jack climbed the beanstalk." She waved her hand to ward off a small cloud of annoying gnats that had gathered around her head. "They're all just fairy tales written to encourage us to be good people. No harm in that, I guess."

Sam's laughter echoed through the barn. "Jack and the Beanstalk?"

"When you have kids and teach kids, sometimes you get your fairy tales mixed up."

"I think they're more than fairy tales." Sam sat down on his folding chair and crossed his arms. "Tell me more about Steve."

"Not much to tell," she replied, leaning back against the wall a few feet away. "He loves living here in Walton Center. He's a good lawyer. He makes a good living that got a lot better today." They both smiled. "Between the two of us, we have a comfortable life. We don't need much."

"And he dreamed of having a small town practice, a great wife, kids, even a white picket fence, right?" asked Sam. "Money was never a consideration for him. He imagined Walton Center. His dream was you."

"That's pretty much spot on. Good guesses," she replied. "Long before we met, he dreamed of the idea of me, or someone like me, a small town girl. He grew up dating city girls. I guess we all want something different from what we had growing up. Steve grew up on the north side of Chicago, raised by a single mom. He doesn't remember his father, who walked out on both of them when he was young. He wanted the polar opposite of all that."

Sam was silent for several seconds deep in thought. "And you?" he began, tilting his head in her direction with his eyes locked on hers. "You wanted something completely different like . . . California. The west coast. Life on a beach. Wineries, great weather, a college professorship."

Sandy's eyes narrowed as he described the life she had always dreamed of, and before he had even finished she had leaned forward off the wall. "You dreamed of being a music professor at the University of Santa Clara. You wanted to greet the sun running on the beach each morning and spend your days teaching woodwinds and instructing the local drum and bugle corps color guard."

Sandy scrunched her brow and tilted her head to one side. "How do you know all that?"

Sam shook his head. "Not exactly sure. I think you told me once while we were working."

"No I didn't."

Sam sucked in a deep breath and exhaled. "Well, you must have. How else could I know such things?"

Sandy nodded slowly. "I guess now you are the only person who knows besides Tracey, and you walked out without meeting her —which was rude, by the way."

"Sorry about that. She wasn't ready to meet me on equal terms."

"I guess not," admitted Sandy.

"So Steve pretty much got what he wanted out of life," continued Sam. "What about you?"

"Look around!" she exclaimed, holding her arms out while she moved in a slow circle gesturing at her summer reality.

"Do you regret your life?"

"How could I say yes? That's an unfair question," she complained. "I have two beautiful daughters. As much as I don't like living in Walton Center, I love my job." She stared at her dirty palms, pondering her next words. "Now I'm just part of someone else's dream. Mine won't ever be fulfilled. I thought I had accepted that. . . " Her voice trailed off into silence.

Sam wiggled the fingers of both hands as if he was waving to himself. "Come on," they urged her, "tell me the rest of it."

"Steve's a good man." She stared into the rafters and began walking as she talked. "A really good man. And a good lawyer. He's always busy helping people. He's good for our community. And my daughters, well they are just the two most amazing girls on the planet. Good students, too. They stay busy. Hang around with good kids." She bent down to tie one of her tennis shoes. "I miss them when we're apart." She paused again when she stood up. "Hey, would you like to come for dinner one night? I'd love you to meet my family." She waited for a response that never came, and turned around to find only an empty chair.

A sudden urge to be with her family washed over her.

Chapter 14

The phone rang a sixth time. Sandy ignored it and carried the groceries inside and placed them on the kitchen island. Only Tracey would let it ring this long.

"Hello, Tracey."

"Hey, Shadow, how'd you know it wasn't your tall, dark and handsome stranger calling?"

"Because he just did," she teased. "Besides, he rings once then hangs up, counts to five, and calls again."

"What? Are you serious?"

"Heavens no, silly," laughed Sandy, shifting the phone to her shoulder and holding it in place with a tilted head so she could work on the first bag of groceries. "Have you forgotten you were my maid of honor?"

Tracey exhaled. "You made me nervous there for a minute."

"Anyway," continued Sandy, "he doesn't show any interest in me, at least not in that way. In some kind of weird way I don't understand, though, I think we're becoming friends."

"Just watch your step," cautioned Tracey. "I've said it before. I don't think a man and a woman can rendezvous in an old barn every day and not get into some kind of relationship. And this guy is a mysterious hot stranger who seems to care about you at a time in your life where you may have some emotional weakness." She paused before adding, "He could take advantage of you."

Sandy rolled her eyes as she emptied the second grocery bag, removing a bottle of merlot and studying its ruby color in the light of the window. "Thanks for your concern but I'm not emotionally weak."

"Are you sure?"

"Did you call for any purpose or just to harass me?"

"Harassment is my specialty," laughed Tracey. "What's up tonight?"

Sandy had a corkscrew halfway into the bottle. "Steve was going to bring home some pizza, but I left a little early and decided to cook a nice meal for him and the girls—who may or may not remember me. We're celebrating! Steve won his big case!"

"I heard!" shouted Tracey so loud Sandy nearly dropped the phone. "It's all over town. Tell him congratulations!"

"I should have known everyone in town already knew." Sandy filled a goblet with wine and stuck the cork back in the bottle, shifting the phone back to her left hand. "And yes, I'll tell him, Tracey. Thanks."

She hung up and took a large gulp from her glass, washing it around her mouth before swallowing it slowly. If she didn't love Tracey so much she'd have to kill her.

When the phone rang again Sandy snatched it off the wall. "What now?"

"Huh? Mom?"

"I'm sorry, Emiley, I thought it was Tracey."

"No problem. May I bring someone home to eat with us tonight?"

"Sure. Who?" asked Sandy.

"Just a boy from school. Just a friend."

"Does this boy friend he have a name?"

"Mom!" screeched Emiley, "he's not a boyfriend!"

"I'm just repeating you," teased Sandy as she took another sip from her glass and began pulling spices down from the cabinet. "Does this boy, who is only a friend, have a name?"

"Bill."

"Bill Buck?"

"Don't make a federal case out of it. Geez, Mom."

"You know, Bill's a drummer, right?"

"Mom! You gotta' stop judging my friends by their choice of musical instruments."

"Dinner is at six. Don't be late."

Steve pulled into the driveway the same time Emiley and her guest arrived.

"Hi, Em," Steve said as he climbed out of his truck. He nodded and smiled at her friend. "Bill, right? Are you having dinner with us tonight?" He placed his hand on the boy's back and turned him toward the front door."

Emiley prodded Bill's arm with her elbow. "Uh, yes, sir."

Steve caught his eye and winked at the boy. "Ouch. I'm afraid that elbow may leave a bruise, Bill."

"Dad!" shouted an embarrassed Emiley.

"Something smells better than pizza!" exclaimed Steve as they walked into the house.

"Hi everyone!" Sandy's enthusiastic welcome bellowed from the kitchen. Wearing a red "Kiss the Cook" apron and holding a glass of wine in one hand and a soup ladle in the other, Sandy peeked around the wall and nodded toward the dining room. "Come on in!"

The table had been set with red china plates and matching cloth napkins. Three white pillar candles were flickering in the center.

"What's the special occasion, Mom?" Emiley glanced at her mom and then settled her questioning eyes on her father.

"It's always special when my family is at home," she announced. "And we're celebrating your dad's court victory!"

Steve's wide grin slowly faded when he spotted the empty bottle of wine on the sideboard. "Where's Sarah?" He glued a smile back on his face.

"Changing her clothes."

"May I speak to you for a moment, honey?" asked Steve.

Sandy brushed off the request. "Not right now. The food will get cold."

Steve gently gripped Sandy's forearm and pointed toward the kitchen with his other hand. "Just for a second."

Sandy pulled away. "Not right now! Geez Steve," she said too loudly for the small room and the situation "Come to the table, everyone!"

"What's wrong with your voice, Mom?" asked Emiley. "You sound like you're . . ."

Steve cut off his daughter. "That's enough, Emiley." His tone made it clear he was serious.

"Supper ready?" ask Sarah as she entered the dining room. "I am soooo hungry." She stopped and looked around from face to face. "What's wrong?"

"Sandy," Steve urged softly. "Let's step into the bedr…"

"Let go of my arm!" she shouted, jerking her limb away. Once free, Sandy reached for the blue and white china bowl of homemade potato leek soup sitting on the sideboard. "Come on everyone, sit!"

Emiley cast a pleading glance at her dad, who offered a slight understanding nod in return. "I guess we better do as the cook says," he announced. "What can I do to help?"

"Why is mom acting so weird?" Sarah whispered to her sister. Emiley just shook her head but remained silent.

Sandy was carrying the soup to the table when she tripped on the edge of an Oriental rug and fell forward, striking her chin on the corner of the table. The bowl smashed into several pieces on the floor, spilling soup everywhere. Some of the hot soup splashed onto Emiley and Bill. Both jumped up and danced around while pulling their steaming clothes away from their skin.

"Sandy!" Steve was at her side immediately, cradling as she slowly sat up. A bruise was already visible on her chin. "Are you okay?"

Sandy nodded once, shook her head vigorously, and then buried her face in her hands and cried.

Chapter 15

Please, God. Let it all have been just a bad dream.

Sandy covered her eyes with her left hand, blocking out the sunlight.

He

With her right, she reached for Steve but found his side of the bed empty.

Loves

The sheets were cold. Had he even slept with her last night?

You…

Sandy threw off the covers and sat up slowly. A rolling sensation as if she was on a cruise ship navigating a rough sea washed over her. Her head pounded, her tongue stuck to the roof of her mouth like a ball of dry cotton, and her stomach churned. Like a newborn foal standing on shaky legs, she eased her way to the bathroom while holding onto the wall with one hand.

One look in the mirror was all she needed to confirm her memory of the evening before. She touched her bruised chin with her left pinky. Tears welled up and spilled down her cheeks as the events of the previous evening assaulted her. How could she have humiliated herself like that? How could she have embarrassed her family?

An hour later, Sandy sat in her car in the gravel parking lot next to the barn, willing herself to climb out and get to work. The Tylenol hadn't helped much, and her chin was throbbing in unison with her head. The day was already warm and promised to be another scorcher. The barn would be an oven. And then her gaze fell to the passenger seat and the new letter from the Illinois Department of Revenue. Steve had managed to get a 20-day extension for the auction, but even that would probably not give her enough time to finish. With a sigh, Sandy climbed out of her car and entered the barn.

She spent a few minutes taking stock of what had been done, and all that still needed to be accomplished. Other than a pair of noisy barn swallows fighting amongst the rafters and the hum of a few invisible insects, silence was the only thing she heard. Walking back toward the front, she rounded pile of bags and boxes with the frame of an old bike sticking out between them, but her hopes were dashed when she realized Sam's chair was still empty. She could have used a friend today.

"How're you feeling?" Sandy shot a look toward the door and tried to maintain her expectant smile when she realized it was Steve.

"Oh. It's you."

"Were you expecting someone else?"

"No, I thought…"

He cut her off. "I know what you were thinking or, I should say, who you were expecting. Steve walked into the barn and scanned its interior. "You're getting it done." He nodded his approval.

"It sure doesn't feel like it." Sandy shifted her position to continually face her husband as he walked down the center of the barn, and then around through a channel she had cleared through the stocks before finally returning to face her in front of the empty folding chair.

The jagged beams of sunlight shooting into the barn captured a haze of hanging dust particles. Steve tried unsuccessfully to stifle a cough. "So, where's this Sam?"

"I have no idea."

"I'm curious," he continued, ducking his head and shooing away a horse fly. "What does he do? Just . . . roll in and help you?"

"Sometimes." Sandy swallowed hard. What was he getting at? "But he's really no help at all. Mostly we talk."

"And I'm supposed to be okay with this?" Steve whipped around to look at his wife. "If he doesn't help, what does he do?"

"I just told you. We talk. I work and he sits over there," she replied, pointing at the empty folding chair against the wall.

Steve walked to the folding chair. "Here? He sits here?"

Sandy nodded. "Yes."

With his eyes locked on his wife, Steve leaned over, ran his index finger across the seat of the metal chair, and held it up in front of her face. It was covered with dust. "He sits in this chair? This one?" pressed Steve, his dirty finger pointing downward.

A small ripple of anger welled inside Sandy when the implication of his words and actions became clear. "I told you he does. You don't believe me. It's dusty in here, Steve." She walked to the nearest carton, rubbed her finger across it, and showed him the result. "This was clean yesterday."

Steve leaned back against the wall and rubbed his forehead with his hand but said nothing.

"Honey, I'm sorry about last night," offered Sandy.

"Whatever happened goes way beyond last night," shot back Steve. "I think we may need some help." He turned and walked out.

Sandy was about to call for him to stop when her mouth fell open in stunned silence. Sam was sitting in the chair staring at her. She closed her eyes tightly and used the base of her hands to rub them hard. When she opened them, the chair was empty.

Oh my God. Am I losing my mind?

Chapter 16

The next few days were filled with work, exhaustion, and stress. Lots of stress.

Steve barely spoke to her, even when they were alone. He made it a point to leave the house before she did, and return home after dinner. The girls completely ignored their mom, Emiley especially, who considered Sandy's "performance art" so embarrassing she was certain that no boy would ever set foot in their house again.

Sandy was washing a few dishes in the sink when the phone rang. She picked it up in the middle of the second ring. "Hello."

"Ready for drum corps, Shadow?"

Sandy shifted the phone to her left ear so she could use the towel in her right to wipe down the counter. "It's a bad idea, Tracey. Steve has barely spoken to me since I fell. The last thing he wants is to spend time with me right now."

"Tell him to get over it," replied her friend. "So you were a little drunk and disorderly. He has more compassion for some of his criminal clients than he does for his wife who had a glass or two of wine while making him a first class meal."

"I'm going to try to speak with him later."

"I'll straighten him out!" interjected Tracey.

"It's not that simple," explained Sandy.

"Sure it is! He's a man!" Tracey continued. "Communication isn't their strong suit unless they're telling us how to fix something. Why can't they just listen? Women have evolved since the cave days. Men? They're still Neanderthals. Know what I'm saying?" Without waiting for a reply, Tracey rushed on. "Big strong bodies. Tiny little brains. A scientific fact. Feed me. Take care of my needs. 'Have something you need fixed? I'll get my club and beat it into submission for you—after the football game.' They just don't get it!" she added, finally taking a breath. "I pity them. Seriously. I really do."

"But that doesn't change my reality," answered Sandy. "I just don't think he's up to being in the same car with me all the way to Dekalb—and vice versa. And . . . we would have to listen to Steve's endless happy talk about the Cubs."

"Tough. I bought the tickets, and all four of us are going. We're headed to a drum corps competition at Huskie Stadium. Dang! I wish we were still eighteen and marching. I'd love to put on the red and black and pull that shako down over my eyes one more time. Vanguard forever, Shadow. Remember?"

Sandy stopped cleaning and sighed. "Oh, how I remember. Easier times."

"Rob and I will pick you guys up four-thirty this afternoon. Wear your red and black!"

Sandy and Steve dressed for the trip to Northern Illinois University's Huskie Stadium engulfed in an uneasy silence. Dressed in white shorts and a red shirt with the Vanguard crest over her heart and "Alumni" embroidered on her left sleeve, Sandy surveyed herself in the full-length mirror on the master bedroom door.

"Are you really wearing that?" Steve asked when he walked around the corner from their bathroom shoes in hand and sat on the edge of the bed.

"What's wrong with it?" She turned her back to the mirror and glanced over her shoulder.

"You're forty," he grunted as he bent over and slipped on his brown loafers. "You were in that silly band when you were a teenager. I don't care what you wear, but your ongoing devotion to this Vanguard thing is like me still being devoted to my little league team." Steve stood up and began walking out of the bedroom.

"Drum and bugle corps. Not band," she shot back. "There's a huge difference, you know." Sandy picked up her compact Canon camera, tossed it into her canvas tote, and followed Steve out to the living room. "Cruelty doesn't fit you," she said coldly. "Maybe I'm not the one with the problem."

He turned and brushed his finger across the fading bruise on her chin. "It's not me sporting one of these."

"I can certainly arrange one for you!" she hissed through clenched teeth, balling her fingers into a fist.

"Mom!" shouted Emiley as she ran out of her bedroom. "What's gotten into you lately? It's like I don't even know you anymore! Stop yelling at Dad! He didn't do anything wrong."

"It's okay, Em," said Steve as he put a hand on her shoulder and escorted her back to her room. "And don't talk to your mother that way," he added, kissing her head as she walked in and closed the door behind her.

"So that's the new game?" spat Sandy, sarcasm dripping from each word. "Humiliate mom in front of our girls?"

"What are you talking about?" asked Steve with both palms turned sideways. "I was supporting you—not undermining you."

"Your chariot awaits!" Tracey shouted as she barged into the kitchen.

Steve picked up his Ray-Bans from the coffee table, walked heavily into the kitchen and past Tracey without a word.

"Well, hi there, Tracey, so glad to see you," she exclaimed.

Steve stopped on the porch and turned around. "Sorry, Tracey. Hello. I'm guessing Rob's in the car?"

"Yup. He's chomping at the bit to hear music in motion." She rolled her eyes.

"Yeah, me too," he replied turning away and making for the driveway.

Tracey pulled off her oversized white sunglasses. "What did I just walk into?"

"Nothing," replied Sandy. "Let's just go."

By the time they turned north onto Highway 47 just a few miles outside town, two very different conversations filled the red Toyota Camry. Sandy and Tracey, occupying the back seat, talked about nothing but music, while Rob and Steve dissected the Chicago Cubs' ongoing season.

"Santo is the best color commentator in baseball," said Steve. "The guy knows the game and describes it in no-nonsense detail."

"It's a crime he's not in the Hall of Fame," replied Rob. "He's the best ballplayer in the history of the game that's still not in the Hall."

"He'll get in. Someday. The baseball writers will come to their senses."

"That's three Santo mentions so far," whispered Tracey, who poked Sandy in the ribs in an effort to get her to loosen up.

"You know, Steve, I was thinking," said Sandy as she leaned forward over the back of his bucket seat. "You worship a team that hasn't won the World Series in nearly a century. Seems to me like maybe it's time to grow up."

Rob shot a look at his friend, but Steve didn't reply or even turn his head. An uncomfortable silence filled the car, punctuated by the rhythmic thump . . . thump . . . thump of the tires hitting the seams in the road.

"You sure know how to kill a conversation," whispered Tracey. Sandy looked out the window. No one spoke another word until they pulled into the Huskie Stadium parking lot at Northern Illinois University.

"Look at this!" exclaimed Rob as he slowly navigated through a jammed lot looking for a place to park. "People are tailgating like it's a football game! We should've brought the grill!"

The other three occupants nodded their heads. "It's better than a football game or any sporting activity," offered Sandy. "Drum Corps is a sport for the arts."

The fans and families of all the competing units—The Phantom Regiment, Madison Scouts, Colts and Glassmen, and, of course, The Vanguard alumni—occupied the parking lot. The smell of charcoal, chicken, hot dogs, and burgers filled the air, as did good-natured ribbing between the rival groups. It was easy to tell corps loyalty by the style and color of the clothing. Groups wearing red and white grilled next to clusters of supporters wearing green and black, navy and silver, blue and white. Nearby, every group's inevitable corps flag had been run up a pole or attached to a line and rippled in the hot summer breeze. It was the same in every direction, as far as the eye could see.

Somehow Rob found a parking spot. As soon as they climbed out, a small group gathered around a Vanguard flag thirty feet behind them screamed, "Shadow! Tracey!" The girls rushed to greet their friends. Steve rolled his eyes. Rob looked bored.

"I didn't think The Vanguard was still around," joked Rob.

"They're not," Steve answered. "I think they disbanded in the mid-seventies due to lack of funding, but this group doesn't seem to want to give it up."

Rob assumed a more serious look. "Come on, Steve, let's get in the spirit. We're not here for us. It's important to our wives. They love this stuff. We can tolerate it for one evening, for them—right?"

"We've had a rough summer, Rob. And it's getting worse by the day."

'What do you mean?" Rob suddenly looked uncomfortable.

Steve shrugged. "You know Sandy's cleaning Tom's old pole barn." Rob nodded. "Let's just say she's not handling it well."

"How so?" Rob asked. Both men watched as their wives laughed with a cluster of told friends and other Vanguard alumni.

"She's spending every day in that barn, allegedly cleaning."

"Allegedly?" A frown creased Rob's head. "Counselor, I know what 'allegedly' means."

Steve looked off into the distance at nothing in particular. "I'm just not sure much work is getting done. And I'm not sure she's alone."

"And I'm not sure what you're insinuating, buddy. It sounds like you're implying Sandy's cheating on you? No way!" Rob exclaimed as he shook his head. "No way!" Steve's only reply was a long glance straight down at his loafers. "I think whatever you two are fighting about may be clouding your judgment," Rob added. "I'll ask Tracey. She'll tell me what's going on."

"Give me a break." Steve's laugh sounded forced. "Those two are closer to each other than they are to us." Steve grimaced and made a V sign. "We're not part of their Vanguard cult, remember?"

The girls returned a few second later, bubbly with excitement and joy. "We haven't seen some of these people in almost twenty years!" exclaimed Sandy. She said it looking at Rob and avoiding her husband's gaze.

"We wanted to introduce you to our friends," said Tracey with her hands on her husband's shoulders. "Why didn't you two come over?"

"We were talking." Rob glanced at his watch when a cacophony of sounds comprised of groups of marching percussionists warming up to prepare for the evening competition reached their ears. "We should probably head into the stadium."

"Ah, there's nothing like the sound of a corps drum line warming up, is there Shadow?" asked Tracey. "Still stirs my soul. Come on guys, let's go find our seats."

Sandy had no intention of sitting anywhere near Steve, and once inside and at their row, she watched where he sat down and plopped herself down three seats over, leaving Tracey and Rob to occupy the middle two.

Once the competition began, the pageantry of the event captivated the women, who talked, cheered, and relived their youth through the young musicians marching on the field.

During The Phantom Regiment performance, a man down below on the track caught Sandy's attention as he watched and loudly cheered the corps. She could not take her eyes off him. He seemed . . . oddly familiar. An audible gasp passed her lips when she figured it out: It was her father, only twenty-five years earlier. The crowd noise morphed into an indistinguishable roar as a memory from 1970 scrolled across her mind. She was fifteen again, marching across a similar field, with her father's hands in the air cheering her on from the sidelines. His actions made it obvious that he loved seeing her in uniform. He was screaming like she was a rock star. When she finished and marched off the field, Tom Loucks ran over and hugged her as tightly as his arms would allow. Tears clung to the corners of her eyes. The pride she remembered feeling from that day long ago was overwhelming in its embrace. She had never again experienced that same emotion, at least not as intensely, as she had on that once-forgotten summer evening.

Finished with its performance, The Phantom Regiment began marching off the field. Sandy held her breath, waiting to see what would happen next. The man locked in her gaze ran to embrace a corps member carrying a sabre. At that, she burst into tears, jumped up from her seat, and ran past the others and down the stairs toward the stadium exit.

"Shadow!"

Tracey stood up, but Steve grabbed her arm. "I'll handle this," he said firmly before walking briskly down the stairs.

Tracey started to follow him but Rob stood to block her way. "Stay here, Tracey. This isn't our business."

Tracey shot her husband a look of incredulity. "What? She's my best friend!" She shoved her way past Rob and flew toward the exit.

Steve caught up with his pacing wife outside the stadium. Tears were streaming down her face.

He grabbed her by the shoulders and gently shook her. "What is wrong with you?" he demanded. "I'm trying to understand, but you're acting like you've lost your mind!"

"Stop!" Tracey yelled as she ran toward them. "Stop it right now!" She pushed her way between Steve and Sandy. "Steve, leave your wife alone! She is going through a lot right now!"

Steve stepped back and raised his hands, palms out, in mock surrender. "You know what? Maybe you've both slipped over the edge."

"Hey, buddy!" Steve turned to see Rob trotting in their direction while motioning to him to meet him halfway. "That's my wife you're talking to. And you shouldn't be talking to your wife that way!" Rob paused before adding, "I think your wife is grieving."

A shocked look passed over Steve's face. "Sandy? Grieving for Tom Loucks? No," he shook his head. "I'm sorry. I didn't mean to—" He threw up his hands and began walking back toward the car.

"Go with him, Rob." Tracey jerked her head toward Steve. "Calm him down. I'll stay here." She turned to an obviously distraught Sandy and opened her arms. "Come here, Shadow. What's going on?"

"I . . . don't . . . know," she said between sobs. "There was a man on the track. He looked like . . . I thought . . . He looked just like my dad did when we used to march."

Tracey held her tight while she cried. "The man did look a little like your father back in the day," confirmed her friend, "but it wasn't him, Shadow. It wasn't him."

"I know, of course it wasn't him," she sputtered, "but when he hugged that girl . . . it reminded me . . . just for a moment. I don't know. For a split second, I thought it was him."

"Grief is powerful, Shadow. You act like you hate him, but the truth is something different. Rob's right, you know." Tracey paused a moment to straighten some of Sandy's hair. "You still haven't allowed yourself to grieve. There's no right way or wrong way to do it, but this, well none of this seems healthy. Not one bit of it."

Sandy melted into Tracey's arms and cried as if her tears could wash away years of disappointment and frustration.

Chapter 17

Steve tried to focus on the brief he was editing, a small piece of the large pile of work stacked on the right side of his desk. He still enjoyed editing in longhand, but unable to find the right word, and having scratched out several, he threw his pencil down in disgust and leaned back in his chair. The silver-framed 8 x 10 photograph of his family taken the previous spring, upright and proper on the opposite desk corner, used to produce a deep smile and a sense of satisfaction that helped him finish his work. Today it distracted his every thought and lodged a weight inside his chest he was unable to shake off.

He had spent the morning arguing with a probation officer, the prosecutor, and the judge that his client deserved to get his driver's license back and be placed on informal probation. The argument was a little unsettling even for Steve, but every client deserves honest and capable representation—and this man had surely paid his dues. Early on in this case, the client's wife had tearfully confided that her husband began drinking years ago. A single beer once a week progressed to one beer a night, and then wine and hard alcohol.

For the last two years he rarely went to bed without a drink on his nightstand. "His habit," she explained, "was a slippery slope that began innocently, but slowly progressed until it was out of hand. It hurt all of us."

"All of us" meant not only his client, but his wife and their three teenage children. A few months earlier, an Illinois State Trooper pulled him over when he failed to use his turn signal. The routine traffic stop for a minor violation turned into handcuffs, the impounding of his vehicle, a DUI charge, and the loss of his license. The good husband and family man with no previous criminal record was also on the verge of being out of a job. He was a pilot, recently promoted to captain for a major airline. Pilots with DUIs risk losing their ability to work. His was a first offense, but his blood alcohol level was double the legal limit and he had refused to cooperate. Neither the FAA nor his airline took those matters lightly. Getting the court to reinstate his driver's license and drop active probation requirements would go a long way toward helping him keep his job. The judge took the matter under advisement and told Steve he would render a decision within a few days.

He had done his best and it was now in the hands of the judge. What Steve could not shake, however, were the similarities between his client and his wife. The more he compared them, the more unsettling they became. Sandy started drinking the same way a few years earlier. One glass of wine here, one vodka grapefruit there, until it was more common to find her with a glass in her hand than it was to see it empty. He was more than a little surprised that her drinking had not yet interfered with her job as a teacher. But he also knew that could change in an instant.

Sandy had never been pulled over for as much as a speeding ticket, but she was a teacher in a small town. He knew that if she were ever found guilty of drunk driving, surviving the damage that would inflict upon her credibility and reputation as a teacher would be nearly impossible. Even an arrest without a conviction could sink her, and teaching was her entire life. Few in the community knew Sandy drank at all. It would only be a matter of time before Bill Buck's parents shared the story of their son's unfortunate dinner at the Richards' home.

In a small town—especially in a small town—perception is reality. He knew he had to do something, and soon, but Sandy was not in the mood to hear anything he had to say. He also knew that as her best friend, Tracey was the key to getting Sandy to understand the seriousness of the situation. But he and Tracey were also barely on speaking terms.

With a final glance at the family portrait, Steve pulled out his cell, punched in the number, and waited for the phone to ring.

"Hello?"

"Hi, this is Steve." The phone was silent for several seconds. "Hello?"

"Everything okay?" she finally asked.

Steve sighed. "Yes. Well, no. Sandy need's your help. It's important." He hesitated before adding, "Our family needs your help, Tracey."

"Has something else happened?"

"Nothing new," he replied, "but her drinking problem, frankly, is out of hand. I know she is wrestling with her dad's death, and her broken relationship with him." He paused to hear her reply, but Tracey remained silent. "She's also seeing someone who probably isn't there. I think you know what I mean."

"Yes. I think I know what you mean."

"I don't know if it's more one than the other," he added. "Probably a combination of all of that."

"What would you like me to do, Steve?"

"I can't explain it. The man at the drums corps competition looked exactly like my father. For a moment I thought it really was." Sandy stomped down an empty cardboard box and set it on a stack of flattened containers. "And Steve's reaction frightened me. He's never been that angry, not at me, anyway."

Sam, who was sitting in the rusty brown folding chair along the front of the barn wall, cocked his head and turned his ear toward the open barn door. "What do you want me to tell you, Sandy?"

"How about that I am not going crazy?"

"Do you think you are losing touch with reality?" he asked. Sandy remained silent, staring at her friend as if begging for an answer. Sam looked toward the door and Sandy followed his gaze. "At times like these, I think it is best to remain calm and just listen."

As if on cue, Steve stepped into the barn.

"What are you doing here?" she asked. Steve stepped several paces into the barn, with Tracey behind him. Sandy took two full steps backward.

Tracey waved her hand as if to make light of their visit. "Hi, girlfriend. You know we both love you. We just want to talk—and you're always here working, so . . ."

"What do you want to talk about?" she asked warily.

Tracey winked in reply and cocked her head toward Steve as if to say, "This is his idea, so I will let him go first."

Sandy slowly turned and looked at Sam, who was seated in his chair nodding his head as if everything would be alright. She turned back to face Steve. "Well? Just say it. You're both here for a reason."

"Okay, I will," he replied. "I believe your drinking has gotten steadily worse in the past couple months and is affecting your judgment. I think your anger toward your father isn't a normal reaction to his death. In fact, I think I grieve more for him than you do." He paused and took a deep breath. "I think you are under a lot of stress—we both know that—and you are . . . hallucinating."

"You've got to be kidding me!" she replied. Her loud forced laugh that came next went on several seconds too long, echoed through the rafters, and prompted several barn swallows into uneasy flight. She looked at Sam for assurance. He was still sitting in his chair at the front of the barn against the wall, leaning forward with his elbows on his thighs, his chin cupped in his hands. "Hallucinating?" she continued. "Maybe I'm not the one with the problem, Steve." An uncomfortable silence followed.

"Tracey—you don't believe all this, do you?" asked Sandy. Her friend bit her bottom lip and looked at Steve for guidance.

"Sandy, you need more help than I'm qualified to give," replied Steve. "I can see this wasn't a good idea." Steve spun on his heels and walked out of the barn.

"Shadow, I'm . . . "I'm sorry," whispered Tracey, who turned and followed Steve.

Sandy, with one hand on her hip and her mouth wide open, spat, "I am not crazy! I think he needs help, Sam. I'm worried about my husband."

Sam offered a small shrug in reply but never took his eyes off the door.

Chapter 18

"It was as if darkness had permeated my skin and entered my soul. I was driven to be somewhere, but had no idea why or where I was headed. I just felt pulled by some invisible force. I was breathing like a panting animal." In her right hand was paper cup of cold water. She took a small sip before continuing. "I felt my bare feet on the ground, cold and wet and I was walking, my steps long and fast. But I had no control of my legs. Then there was nothing under my feet and I fell into a pit of some kind, a long slow drop into darkness."

"Were you afraid?"

"No. I don't think so. My landing was soft. I looked up. I saw the outline of the top of the pit. Beyond was only darkness. I was confused, but I wasn't afraid. It was like all my senses were heightened. I heard muffled sounds of people talking, but I couldn't understand what they were saying. I didn't recognize their voices. I had no communication or contact with anything. My vision began to go blurry. I was enveloped in some sort of . . . sack. It wasn't paper or plastic. It wasn't hot or cold. It felt the same temperature as my body. I couldn't tell where I ended, and where the opaque cocoon began."

The therapist sat back in her green leather chair and, using a yellow pencil, wrote a few notes on her pad. She looked to be about 50, tall, with silver hair spilling onto her shoulders. A pair of reading glasses hung loosely about her neck on a thin silver chain. She had a kind warm smile, and voice to match. "Go on," she urged softly.

Sandy continued. "Even though I couldn't get out, I sensed, more than I knew, that outside the sack or bag or cocoon, my life was . . . out of control. Inside, I was safe. And then I woke up."

"And?" asked the therapist.

"And nothing. I woke up."

The therapist was quiet for several seconds. "How did you feel when you realized you were awake?"

"Sad." She glanced toward the door just ten feet away.

"If you had to use three more adjectives to tell me how you felt knowing you were awake, what would they be?"

Sandy thought a moment. "Frustrated. Overwhelmed. And . . . lost."

"Why did you feel this way?"

"Because all the things I had been dealing with were still waiting for me in the real world. I wanted to fall back into that warm darkness again, into the cocoon. I wish I were there now."

"That's pretty common, Sandy," she said in her soft comforting voice. "What do you think your dream meant?"

Sandy frowned. "You're the shrink. Isn't that what my husband is paying you to figure out?"

"How much did you drink before bed the night you had the dream?"

"I'm not an alcoholic!" shot back Sandy. "And I know alcoholics. My father was one. For many years. And since I'm not, we can move on." She looked at the door again. I wonder if it's locked.

"I didn't say you are," replied the therapist in a calm, steady voice. "But alcohol, even small amounts, alone or with medications, can have a profound effect upon how we sleep, how and what we dream, how we perceive our day-to-day life." She paused before adding, "If you know alcoholics, then you know what I am telling you is true."

"I suppose."

"You can leave, Sandy," added the therapist. "I can't keep you here and I would not try. My hope is that you came to see me because you believe that I can help you."

Sandy nodded. "I promised my husband I would come."

"How much did you drink before bed?"

"One glass of red wine."

"When was the last time you didn't have wine before bed?"

Sandy raised her hand with an open palm. "I don't drink every night."

"I believe you. When was the last night you didn't have wine before going to bed?"

"I don't know," huffed Sandy as she folded and unfolded her legs and shifted about in the chair in an effort to get more comfortable. "Tell me, doc, do you have heart disease in your family?" When the therapist didn't reply, she asked again. "Well? Do you? Doctors recommend wine, particularly red wine. One glass per day is supposed to reduce the risk of heart disease."

The therapist jotted another note.

"Write this down, doc. While you're having open heart surgery, I'll be having my nightly glass of wine."

"Sandy, let's talk about why you came today," suggested the therapist, who folded her hands atop her yellow pad and smiled. "I like the way you shared your dream with me—that is very helpful. But you are showing anger with me, and you keep glancing toward the door. As I said, and as you know, you came voluntarily, and you can leave whenever you wish."

"I promised my husband I'd see you. And my best friend." Sandy lifted her paper cup to her lips and drained it. "And here I am."

"Will you share with me why they thought it was important for you see a therapist?"

Sandy sighed deeply, looked up at the ceiling, and then back down at her hands. "I had an incident." Her lower lip quivered. "I embarrassed my family."

"What happened?"

"My daughter had a friend over for dinner," she began. "I was carrying a bowl of soup to the table and I tripped. The soup went all over my daughter and her friend. And I broke the bowl."

"You tripped or you fell?" The therapist could see tiny tears clinging to the bottom of Sandy's eyelashes.

"I tripped—flat on my face."

"Were you hurt?"

"I bruised my chin," she said, reaching up to point at the spot, "but I destroyed my self-esteem. And my credibility with my family was . . . damaged."

"And that's all?"

"I tripped and fell, isn't that enough?"

The therapist rolled the pencil between her left thumb and forefinger for a few seconds. "Sandy, people usually don't come to see me because they're clumsy."

Sandy re-crossed her legs and looked away. *Steve has probably told this woman everything that has happened in our marriage recently. . . .*

"We were at an event at Huskie Stadium with friends. I became upset and ran out."

"What upset you enough to make you do that?"

"I thought I saw my father."

"Did you?"

"He's dead."

"So you didn't see him?"

"What do you think?"

"It doesn't matter what I think." Sandy remained silent and studied her hands. Now it was the therapist's turn to twist in her seat to become more comfortable. "You were kind enough to allow me to speak with Steve before our session."

Sandy lifted her gaze to meet the therapist's eyes and nodded.

"Tell me about Sam."

Sandy's eyes narrowed, her brow furrowed, and a smirk formed on the corners of her mouth, which refused to speak.

"Your husband shared with me that you often have a daily visitor at your father's barn. And his name is Sam." Fifteen seconds of silence ticked past. "Is your husband misinformed?" More silence.

"Do you hear voices?"

"Just yours."

"Do you hear voices when you're in your father's barn?"

Silence. But the tears rolling down her cheeks spoke volumes.

"Sandy," began the therapist, "I want to talk with you about depression."

Chapter 19

"Slept in today, huh?" Sam asked from his familiar position on his chair when Sandy walked in the next morning.

"Why is it I never see you come in?" Sandy responded more curtly than she had intended. "And how did you get in? You don't have a key."

"Well good morning," he said with his usual warm smile. "You left the door unlocked yesterday."

Sandy thought a moment. "Actually, I'm sure I did not. But what about my first question? You're not here, then you are here. I never see you come in or actually . . . leave. I never see you around town—or anywhere—but here." She put down her small blue cooler with her drinks and a sandwich next to the front wall of the barn and turned back to face him, arms folded across her chest.

"The same could be said of you, Sandy," replied Sam, stretching out his full length on the chair before hooking his hands above his head. "You're either here or you're not, right? It's a matter of perception and, what, physics?"

"You're mocking me and I have no tolerance for it today," she snapped.

"No, I'm not. You weren't here this morning. I was just wondering where you were."

How much do I share with him? "If you must know," she replied slowly, "I was seeing a shrink."

"A what?"

"I think you heard me. I'm seeing a head doctor!"

"Why?"

"I had a little too much to drink a few nights ago and I embarrassed myself."

"Do people see a head doctor because they had a few too many?"

"She asked if I hear voices." When Sam didn't respond, she continued. "Maybe I'm mentally ill . . . or at least someone seems to think I might be."

"Seeing a 'head doctor,' as you call it, doesn't mean you're mentally ill," cautioned Sam.

"You only see an M.D. if you're physically ill, or think you might be sick. Or maybe you're getting a check-up to make sure you're not sick," she explained. "So if I'm seeing a psychologist, I assume it's because I'm emotionally or mentally sick—or someone thinks I am."

"And who might this someone be?"

"I guess that someone is Steve," admitted Sandy. "Tracey thinks I need to 'speak with someone,' too. And you know what else?" she continued. "Steve thinks I'm depressed and seeing things that aren't there."

"Things?" Sam lowered his hands to his thighs.

"People," she said. "Believe it or not, he thinks I'm seeing people. Actually, that isn't quite right. He thinks I'm imagining or inventing a person, you know, in my head."

Sam scrunched his brow as if in thought. "And who might that be, Sandy?"

"I think we both know the answer to that question."

Sam didn't move a muscle or change his demeanor in any way. "What do you think?" he asked softly.

Sandy chewed on the inside of her mouth a moment before answering. "Sometimes I'm not so sure."

"Do you see me now?"

"Stop it. You know what I mean." She lowered her voice. "Do you think I am depressed?"

"It doesn't matter what I think."

"Well do you?" she insisted. "That's the question of the day, isn't it? I mean, look at a quick rundown of my life. I'm not happy I'm spending my vacation cleaning this barn. No, I don't think I'm paralyzed by sadness or doom. Yes, I wish certain aspects of my life were different, but that's life and who doesn't?" she asked, her hands turned up as if pleading her case. "And I don't have trouble getting out of bed in the morning—"

"What about your dad?" interjected Sam. "And the matches?"

Sandy stared at him for a few seconds. "Yes, I'm angry at my dead father. No, I'm not planning to take my life, although there are moments where that option seems, or seemed," she corrected herself, "appealing."

"I'm assuming these are all questions your shrink asked?"

"Don't call her my shrink!" she shot back. "I don't like giving up my summers for this," she continued, gesturing into the depths of the barn, "I'm not crazy, and I'm not depressed. I'm fine. Life is what it is."

"Life is what we make of it," offered Sam.

"Sounds like a lot of positive mumbo jumbo to me," she scoffed.

Sam stood and walked a few steps to a rafter, grabbed it with both hands, and hung for several seconds before letting go. "Most people travel through life focusing on the negative," he said. "What they don't have, or don't own or possess, depresses them. All the failures they think they have endured seem to pile up and life becomes more of a burden. Unhappy or envious people are rarely grateful for their successes or their blessings. Those who expect the worst, usually get it."

"Right," she shot back. "Look at what is all around us on the earth: Disease, famine, abject poverty, sadness, death. It's all unavoidable."

"There will always be sickness and disease," continued Sam. "The poor will always be with us. But, we don't have to give in to it and accept it as our own reality. There is also good health, food in abundance, wealth, and happiness. What you look for, you usually find." He scratched his chin. "Who's your happiest student?"

"What's that have to do with this?" she asked. "Tyler Williams."

"So his family is successful and wealthy."

She shook her head. "Quite the opposite. He comes from a broken home and is being raised by a single mom. He rarely has lunch money."

"How does he eat?"

"I try to make sure he always has enough money for lunch."

"And for shoes?"

"How do you know that?" asked a surprised Sandy.

Sam smiled. "Small town. So Tyler has to rely on the generosity of others and he's the happiest student in school?"

Sandy thought for a moment. "Yes."

"Maybe Tyler chooses to be happy," offered Sam.

"Or maybe he just doesn't know any better," countered Sandy. "What are you trying to tell me?"

Sam shrugged. "I'm just sharing my thoughts on the importance of believing in the best."

"What does that mean?"

"There are some things in life beyond our control. We can't control the weather, for instance, and we can't control the actions of others."

"Well then we agree," announced Sandy. "We have little or no control over life."

"No, we don't agree. You're missing the point entirely."

Sandy sighed. "Then what is your point?" she demanded, placing her hands on her hips while she tossed her hair over her left shoulder. "Sam, I've had it rough lately, and my patience is wearing thin."

"You can't control the actions of others," he said gravely. "But you can control how you react to what others do to you. I am talking about your attitude and your effort, Sandy. Be optimistic and work hard. Look for the best and you'll often find it. Work for the best, and you'll often get it."

Sandy offered a small smile. "My father used to say something like that. Of course," she added, sweeping one of her hands in the air to indicate the extent of the garbage littering the barn, "no one left him with all this crap, a tax lien, and a wasted summer."

"True enough," replied Sam. "But your father had a saying like that because he was an encourager."

"He was anything but," shot back Sandy. "You didn't know him."

Sam shrugged. "I think he was an encourager."

"What could possibly make you think that? You never met him. You know nothing about him."

"He never encouraged you or others?" asked Sam.

"Yeah, maybe. When I was young and growing up."

"Did he change?"

"Can't you see?" she asked. "Look around."

"I think maybe you should look around, Sandy. I think you're confusing this barn with your father. They're not one and the same."

"Of course a barn is not a man!" she scoffed. "What are you talking about?"

"Clean up his building as you are," he suggested, "but while you are at it, look for the man. Look beyond the building."

Sandy shook her head and sighed. "You talk like a therapist, you know?" she asked. "Two shrinks in one day are more than I can handle. I think what I really should do is get back to work." Look beyond the building. Look for the man. "Wait. What are you trying to tell me?

Sam spoke more slowly. "Look . . . beyond . . . the . . . building. Do you see the man? Look for the man . . ."

Sandy stared at him, trying to understand, and then turned toward the waiting stacks of boxes.

"Lots of leaves, Sandy. Boxes and boxes of leaves."

Sandy pulled down an oblong box about three feet long and nearly as wide. Something about it felt different. Dropping it onto the dirty concrete floor, she pulled her box cutter from the back pocket of her jeans, bent over, and quickly opened the top flaps. The odor of decomposing leaves and general rot rose up to greet her. As she did with all the boxes, she used her gloved hands to dig into the content to make sure there was nothing else inside. This time, however, her right hand hit something solid.

Sandy froze.

She kept her right hand in place and dragged her left hand through the contents to discover the same thing. There was something else in the box. Something solid. "Well, I might be imagining lots of things," she joked with herself, "but my hands aren't." Sandy brushed aside several inches of leaves and withdrew what at first glance appeared to be a faded white and brown photo album. In fact, it was a scrapbook. Something tugged at her memory, a faint shimmer of recollection.

Dropping to her knees, Sandy pulled off her gloves and ran her fingertips across the old musty cover. She slowly opened the front cover with one hand while the other supported the weak hinge that looked as though it was ready to fall part. A wave of familiarity washed over.

My Leaf Collection, by Sandy Loucks,
Fourth Grade, Walton Center Grade School

"Oh my," she sighed as she flipped slowly through the pages of pressed leaves and scrollings of a child long since gone.

It was autumn.

A wave of warm recollections nearly overwhelmed her.

A Saturday morning. The air was cold and crisp.

Her father was so excited when he learned about her project. He drove her to the woods to help collect the leaves.

Reds. Oranges. Yellows. Browns. So vivid she could see them still. "Dad put me on his shoulders so I could reach the leaves and pick them."

And then her right hand flew to her mouth in shock when she read the last line she had written, on the last page of the scrapbook: "Someday I will have the largest leaf collection in the whole wide world!"

She read the line over and over as its real meaning slowly dawned upon her.

"Oh my God!" she exclaimed as she slowly stood and looked around her father's barn as if seeing it for the first time. Her eyes came to rest on the giant piles of leaves in the front of the building, dumped from hundreds of boxes and bags.

He was saving them for me.

"My God, it wasn't him at all. It was me."

She pulled the scrapbook to her chest, sat back down, and wept.

Chapter 20

"I'm pleased to see you," smiled the therapist, shaking Sandy's hand and guiding her inside her office. She closed the door gently behind her and motioned for her take a seat on the sofa. "I thought our first session might be our last," she explained as she leaned back in her own chair facing Sandy.

"I almost didn't come back," she admitted, plucking absentmindedly at a shirt sleeve. "But I have been doing a lot of thinking—about my father. I would like to talk about him."

The therapist nodded, wrote something on her notepad, and then sighed. "Sandy, before we go any further, are you aware that I knew your father?"

Sandy's eyebrows shot upward. "You did?"

"Yes. I work part-time for the Veterans Administration. One day a week I see veterans."

"Oh."

"Under normal circumstances, the doctor-patient privilege does not allow me to discuss anything with you. This is generally true even though your father has passed away. However, shortly before your father died, he handed me a letter," she continued, lifting an envelope off the desk for Sandy to see before setting it down again. "I will make a copy for you. It is only one short paragraph that says after his death, I could talk about anything he had to say to me with either Dorothy—his wife, of course—and you."

Sandy offered a puzzled look. "I don't understand."

"Frankly, I don't fully understand either," replied the therapist. "But he knew enough to waive the doctor-patient privilege."

Sandy shook her head. "How could he know I—or my mom—would be here talking with you?"

"That I can't tell you either," she replied, "but it's a small town. There are only two of us here."

Outwardly Sandy remained calm and silent, but inside her mind was racing. Tom Loucks had seen a psychologist?

"The VA encouraged your dad to see me after he was arrested for striking a health department official. I'm sure you remember the event. It made national news, I believe."

"Why are you telling me this," asked Sandy.

"I think understanding his condition may help you better understand yourself." She paused to write a few things on her pad. "How much do you know your dad's military service?"

Sandy shook her head. "Not a thing. He never talked about it."

"I'm not surprised. The World War II vets are a tough bunch. Their war has been glamorized by Hollywood, but reality was altogether different. What those vets saw, what they did, what they endured . . . affected their lives in ways most of them—or most of us—never fully understood."

The therapist lifted her reading glasses, placed them on her nose, opened a manila folder, and studied its contents for several seconds. "Your dad shipped overseas in 1942 and didn't return until the war was over in 1945," she continued. "He didn't see home in three years. Generally speaking, back then you served and fought until the war ended. That was tough on everyone." She flipped another page inside the folder. "Their problems were compounded because most of them refused to talk much about their experiences, even with their families." She paused. "Especially their families. They were products of the Great Depression, hardship, hunger, and being stoic was simply the culture of their generation. As President Kennedy said they were 'born into the great depression, tempered by war.'"

Sandy didn't realize she had leaned forward as if to better hear and understand every word. "I never really thought about any of this."

"He served with the First Infantry Division—'The Big Red One.' Does that name mean anything to you?" she asked. When Sandy shook her head, the therapist added, "It is one of the most famous fighting divisions in the history of America."

"Your dad landed in Algeria on November 8, 1942, as part of Operation Torch," she continued. "He was wounded there, in North Africa, and again in the invasion of Sicily the following July. He saw a lot of action, Sandy. Hard, close, face-to-face, hand grenade-throwing combat. You've seen the movies. You've seen the stories on the news, watched the history specials."

Sandy offered a vigorous nod. "It's very hard to think about. I can't even picture my dad doing any of that."

"But he did. Your father's experiences were horrific, Sandy. After being wounded twice in two campaigns," she continued, "he returned to England with the division to prepare for the invasion of France. He was in the first wave at D-Day on Omaha Beach." She watched as Sandy's mouth slowly fell open. "He survived that horrible day, but about one of every three men around him was killed or wounded. Your dad went on to fight across France to the

German border by September, saw more terrible fighting that fall, and then nearly six weeks more in the Battle of the Bulge, often in freezing weather. He crossed the Rhine into Germany at Remagen, and ended the war in Czechoslovakia."

"I never knew any of that!" Sandy gasped. "How did anyone survive?"

"That in itself is something of a miracle," confessed the therapist. "All of this helped shape the man you would know as your father. I want to return to Omaha Beach and D-Day. Sandy, did you know that your father's best friend died in his arms that morning?"

"Oh dear God," she moaned, her right hand now supporting her forehead as she looked toward the floor. "He never shared that with me," she whispered.

"The death of his friend would have been bad enough, but because of the way it played out, your father believed the bullets that killed his friend were intended for him."

"What does that mean?"

The therapist found the document she was looking for and turned the file around so Sandy could see it was written in her father's handwriting. ". . . Once we made it out of the water, we were running for our lives across the beach for cover. Agno started on my left. I yelled, 'Head to the right, Agno, toward the rocks!' I pulled him in that direction and shoved him ahead of me. He took my place as we moved right, just a head of me. Not much later, maybe fifteen or twenty seconds, I saw his body quiver and his whole upper back was a deep red. He turned to look at me before he collapsed in my arms. I dragged him behind some rocks. I guess by then he was probably already dead. If I hadn't pulled him, hadn't told him where to head, it would have been me who got that bullet."

The therapist peered at Sandy over her glasses. Her face had lost all its color, her eyes brimming with tears. "Are you aware that, many years later, your father struck a fifteen-year-old boy?"

"Yes, I remember. It happened in my father's restaurant."

"Do you know what triggered the incident?"

Sandy nodded. "The boy's German accent." In a moment of epiphany, she jumped from her chair with both hands cradling her face. "That's it! That's why he hated anything and everything to do with Germany."

The therapist nodded. "Like most of his generation, your father didn't differentiate between Nazis and all Germans. In his mind, Germans killed Agno. Sit down, Sandy, there's more." Sandy promptly sat down. "Have you ever heard of the term Post Traumatic Stress Disorder?"

"You mean PTSD?"

"Yes. Our World War Two vets weren't immune to it, although back then they called it Battle Fatigue or Combat Neurosis. Most civilians knew it as shell shock. Sometimes Hollywood gets it fairly right. Have you seen the movie Patton?"

"I know what you are going to say," she replied. "That is my husband's favorite movie. Patton slapped a soldier and called him a 'yellow bastard' for trying to get out of combat duty."

The therapist smiled and nodded. "Actually, we believe he had what we now call PTSD. Getting any veteran to admit to any suffering from any battlefield ailment that didn't involve blood was and remains difficult. In their minds, if it didn't bleed, it wasn't a serious problem. They certainly weren't going to admit to any type of mental or emotional disorder."

"So you're telling me my father had PTSD?"

She nodded. "He brought it home with him from overseas. Not all wounds are visible, Sandy. He didn't see me enough to allow for a complete diagnosis, and he became angry when I even suggested the possibility. Admitting that he might be suffering from some type of mental or emotional disorder is not a weakness. It's a casualty of war as real as any physical wound." She slipped her glasses off her nose and played with the thin chain with her fingers. "But I would bet my license on the fact that your father suffered from PTSD. It got worse over time, and was especially pronounced later in his life."

Sandy shook her head. "I don't understand. Why didn't my mother tell me this?"

"You'd have to ask her," suggested the therapist. "I don't know whether she knew the full extent of your father's service, or what he told her. She had to have known there were problems, but, like all good wives of her generation, she supported her husband's decision not to talk about it. Don't forget," she added, making a scissors with her right hand fingers, "she's cut from the same cloth."

Sandy sighed and looked out the window. It was some time before she spoke. "I really know very little about either of my parents."

"Unfortunately," the therapist replied, "That's not unusual."

"So how does PTSD show in a person?"

"You mean what are its symptoms?" asked the therapist. Sandy nodded. "There are many, and they vary widely. Some people have most or all of the symptoms. Others may only have one or two. PTSD often begins with bad, intrusive memories. Some have flashbacks of traumatic events that can last for a few seconds, several minutes, or even days. Most have what we would call nightmares about the traumatic event that refuses to leave them."

"My father had nightmares, often," replied Sandy. "I remember him waking up and screaming. I recall my mom trying to calm him. Now I know why."

"Even those who don't have regular nightmares often have trouble sleeping," continued the therapist. "Most sufferers feel emotionally numb. That's a way to avoid thinking about what happened to them. They often feel hopeless about the future, suffer memory problems, and have difficulty maintaining close relationships. Anger is another symptom," she added. "In your father's case, I know he had anger management issues and violent outbursts."

"My dad had a lot of anger inside. What else?"

"As I said, it spans the gamut," she admitted. "Some have overwhelming moments of guilt, or shame. There's often self-destructive behavior—drinking too much, drug use. Some suffer from extreme depression, high startle response, and the most sad of all, many veterans suffering from PTSD take their own lives."

"I don't believe my father ever tried to kill himself," replied Sandy, "but he had many of these symptoms."

"Another rather different symptom is one particularly difficult to diagnose with vets of your father's generation. All of them survived the Great Depression, which would certainly make hoarding understandable, with or without PTSD."

Sandy stiffened and her hand flew to her mouth. "I'm sorry, did you say, 'hoarding?'"

"Yes," she replied. "Was your dad a hoarder? I am not talking about just saving a few things."

"I know what you mean," she shot back, nodding her head several times. Warm tears welled up in her eyes.

"I wish your father had come back to see me more often," continued the therapist. "I can tell you this though, from the sessions I had with him and from other documents and notes in his file, I came to respect your father as a genuine American hero. He gave his country the best he had, and he paid a very high price. He left a piece of himself over there just as surely as if he'd lost an arm or a leg."

Taking a Kleenex from the box offered by the therapist, Sandy dabbed her tears. "You said earlier my dad believed his friend was killed by bullets that should have struck him, is that right?"

"Yes. We often call it Survivor's Guilt. There is absolutely no doubt that complicated your father's PTSD."

"He never talked about anyone from the war, at least not to me," explained Sandy. "What did you say his friend's name was? Arnie?"

She flipped through the folder again. "No, it was Agno. A- G- N-O. I don't know if that's a first name or a last. It could have been a nickname." She shook her head. "I'm sorry. I just don't know."

"I'm don't think I ever heard my father mention anyone named Agno."

The therapist looked at her clock and smiled. "This has been a strong and wonderful session, Sandy." She walked her to the door. "With knowledge, comes understanding. Understanding ignites compassion."

Thoughts tumbled and spun in her mind as she walked through the parking lot to her car. She had wasted years misjudging her father. He had done many things wrong—most or all of which were voluntary, but over which he did not have full control. She had never known him at all. She had allowed her benign but obstinate ignorance to hone her reality into an ugly lie.

"Daddy," she cried, weeping now like a small child while gripping the steering wheel until her knuckles turned white. "I'm sorry. I didn't understand. I didn't know what I was doing," she sobbed. "I had no idea what you were going through . . . how you were suffering. I was selfish. I ignored your problems and only focused on mine. I'm sorry, so very sorry. Please forgive me."

As she drove away, she could not get the therapist's final words out of her mind: *"With knowledge, comes understanding. Understanding ignites compassion."*

Chapter 21

"I'm done!"

Sandy's voice echoed through the old pole barn.

Standing in the middle of the enormous structure, she turned a full circle surveying her accomplishment. The mountains of boxes, bags, and debris were gone. Other than bits of cardboard, frayed wads of packing tape, and the occasional candy wrapper, the barn was empty. Thick cobwebs still coated the walls in some places, and vines still grew out of the corners along the wall. They would soon be someone else's problem.

"You think so?" asked Sam.

"Yes, I do," she said without turning around. "I even finished with a few days to spare."

Sam walked toward her from behind, his heavy black boots clicking loudly now that there was nothing inside to absorb the sound. He squatted down when he reached her side, and used his forefinger to doodle in the thin layer of dust and dirt coating the barn floor. "We're on this earth to be servants to each other, Sandy," he said, dragging his finger slowly in a broad semi-circle. "What you're doing, what you've done for your father, is stepping into his place and finishing his work. You're serving him and you're almost finished."

"I have no idea what you are talking about, Sam," she replied.

"Wait. Did you say 'almost?'"

The left corner of his upper lip lifted in a half-smile. "Well, let's just say it's almost complete."

"I went through everything," she insisted. "Look around! I cleaned up his mess."

"Indeed you have," answered Sam. "You cleaned up his mess."

"Is there something else I missed?" When Sam did not reply, she raised her eyebrows and snapped a finger. "Ah, you mean the tax liens. I am one step ahead of you, my friend. That horrible mess is fixed as well. Steve negotiated the original amount to less than half, and they removed all the penalties. We now have the money to pay it ourselves, and Steve volunteered."

Sam rubbed his chin and grinned. "That must be a huge relief. But you have still only cleaned up his mess."

Sandy turned her hands palm up. "I give up."

"We all make messes of our lives to one degree or another," he explained. "We hope we can straighten them out or clean up our mess before it's too late, but sometimes," he stood up and wiped the dust from his hands, "sometimes time runs out. Like a basketball game, the clock of life ticks off the seconds, the minutes, the hours, and the days. And when the buzzer sounds . . ."

Sandy frowned. "You are ruining my good mood, Sam."

"The clock ended before your dad could do all this for himself. That can happen to any of us at any time. Young, old—it doesn't matter. Our time in this life is limited."

"Well of course it is," shot back Sandy. "Who doesn't know that?"

"Knowing is one thing," Sam replied. "But who really believes their own time will be short?" He stared at her for a few seconds, just long enough to make her uncomfortable. "No one knows their time of departure."

"Departure?" Sandy shook her head. "That's an odd word. When we're dead, we're dead. "To 'depart" implies you are going somewhere."

"That's right," he continued. "Our bodies die but our souls go on. We all have to be prepared. Even under the best of circumstances, there will be work left undone."

"My dad had no intention of cleaning up the barn," she continued. "I believed he was busy creating messes for me to clean up. Now I find out he suffered from PTSD and it probably caused most of the problems he suffered after the war." Sandy began walking slowly back to the front of the barn with Sam at her side. "I blamed him for everything that was wrong in our family, Sam. Everything. But everything wasn't his fault. Most of it wasn't. The problem was my own insensitivity and selfishness."

"I don't think you were selfish or insensitive," Sam replied. "You didn't understand, and your father couldn't help his family understand. But of course, he probably had no idea what he was doing to himself or to his family. We all make mistakes large and small, Sandy. All of us. The only thing that matters is that when we do, and when we know, we change."

"I understand that better now," she admitted. "I so regret what I did. For so many years I treated him like he was nothing but a drunk and a bum."

"And now what do you believe?"

"He left all this, and it is still a little confusing," she confessed, "but now I know he left it for me." A pensive look crossed her face. "Yes, I had a tough summer and a lot of stress, and my reward was having to dig through a huge barn, most of it crammed with countless boxes and bags of decaying leaves my dad had been saving—as a gift for me in his own"—Sandy struggled to find the right word—"his own . . . way."

When Sam smiled, Sandy tilted her head and narrowed her eyes. "What's making you smile?"

"You may never think of all this as a reward," he said, waving his hands in the air to take in the empty barn, "but you performed a wonderful and blessed service for your dad and saved your mother from her burdens—the barn, the tax lien, and the pain she carried about how and what you thought of your father."

Sandy's face slowly lit up, as if a sudden realization struck her. "He knew I would figure it out, but he was too ill to fully understand all of what he was putting me through," she said slowly. "But my mother would never have figured it out, and we could not hire it done because strangers would never have figured it out, either." She stopped and watched Sam's smile grow larger. "I was the only one who could have done this."

"The rewards that are the most important in life, aren't of this earth."

At that, Sandy fell silent. She walked along the far wall about halfway down the length of the barn before turning around to face him. "Do you believe there is a God, Sam?"

His gaze locked onto Sandy and drew her closer, step by step. "There is." When she was a few feet from him, he continued. "When we first met, you asked, 'Why would God do this to me?' Do you remember?"

"Yes," she said with a firm nod of her head. "I still wonder that."

"God doesn't do things to people. The better question might be, 'Why would God allow this to happen?' Walk with me, Sandy." Together they slowly made their way toward the front of the barn and from there, began walking around the perimeter, side by side. "God uses all things for His good purpose—if we open our hearts to see it. I think He used this barn and the giant, seemingly insurmountable, mess to do a great work within you."

"Within me?" she asked.

"You're not the same woman I met weeks ago. I believe this old warehouse, or pole barn as you call it, became your instrument of change."

Sandy thought for a few moments before nodding in agreement. "I see that now. I never would have without you." They continued walking, their footsteps echoing off the rough wooden sides of the barn. "Do you believe there is a heaven, Sam?"

He closed his eyes and smiled as if imagining a beautiful place. "As sure as I'm standing here, there's a Heaven."

"Are you here" She turned away so Sam could not see the tears welling up in her eyes. "My husband and my kids think I'm 'emotionally exhausted'—that you are a figment of my imagination. Tracey says I'm hallucinating."

"What do you think?"

She hesitated. "I think you are here." Her words lacked confidence.

"I didn't come here for them. It doesn't matter what they think."

"You came for me?" By this time the tears were running down her cheeks. "You didn't know me."

The mouth of the stranger who had become a friend transformed into a wide smile. "All I can tell you is that one day I was running on a beach, and the next day I was here. Time is relative. I am here now, but not only for you."

Blood rushed to her face. "Then who else are you here for?"

"I am here for him."

Sandy furrowed her brow as her questioning eyes met his. "You're here for Steve?"

"I'm performing a service for a friend. I'm here for Duke."

"Daddy?" Here voice trembled, the word nearly catching in her throat. She hadn't called her father that since she was twelve years old.

"Your dad performed a service for me that I could not perform for myself," replied Sam. "He did it with a joyful heart."

"Wait!" she responded sharply, as if the spell was broken. "I've never seen you around town. How did you know him?" Her eyes narrowed. "Something doesn't add up."

Sam chuckled softly. "Not everything adds up in human measurements. Time is relative, as is age. In this life, you need reference points to measure both. But there is a place where those reference points are meaningless. The soul has no beginning and no end. There is no need to measure. I know you can't understand that now. But you will. Your father was a kind and gentle man. He loved his family. He loved you with a love that is immeasurable."

As she stared into Sam's eyes, all the important and memorable moments she had spent with her father scrolled through her mind. "What's happening to me, Sam?" Her heart raced and the blood pounded in her temples. "What did you do?

"I've done nothing. You've done it all yourself. You are on a beautiful journey. I'm here to help you on your way. You're loved deeply by many, Sandy," explained Sam. "Someday you will come to know that you are surrounded by a great cloud of witnesses. Don't be too self-critical. Your students, your friends, your family . . . you are loved. You make a positive difference in the lives of everyone you touch."

"And we learn even more," sighed Sandy, "sometimes the hard way, from our personal mistakes."

Sam nodded. "We give love and receive love. We must be grateful for the hardships as well as the blessings we encounter along the way. Both pull us closer to complete understanding and love. Our hardships pull us closer to God. So be grateful."

"Am I failing?"

"No. We enjoy small successes and endure small failures along the way." Sam paused to let her soak it in. "But in the big picture, it's all a learning process. Above all, know that you are loved."

A patch of dirt on the floor off to the side caught her eye. She smiled at the little drawing of a fish he had made with his finger. When she turned to face him, he had disappeared. Sandy rushed to the door and looked outside, but he was nowhere in sight.

She turned back and, with a heavy sigh, took stock of the warehouse and all she had accomplished. Somehow, it now looked less complete. The boxes were gone, but the dirt and cobwebs remained. "Okay, Daddy. This is for you," she whispered. "It . . . it was . . . it is, a privilege to serve you. I'm grateful you entrusted this task to me." She didn't fully understand the words that came tumbling out of her mouth, nor was she convinced she was sincere.

Sandy reached for the wide broom leaning against a pillar and went to work. The cobwebs came down in tiny white swirls, spooling around the long broom handle as she reached and wiped as high as she could reach. She swept the dirt and debris into a score of small piles before scooping them, one by one, into an empty box. With a new-found energy, she cleaned as if the barn were her new home.

Two hours later, the floor was clean and most of the cobwebs gone, but Sam's little fish remained intact. Dirty and tired, she walked to the front of the barn by the door and was about to turn off the lights when a memory of the day her father purchased the warehouse filled her mind. She and her dad walked through his building. She remembered being so proud of her daddy. The love she'd felt for him flooded over her, just as it had when Sam had been talking about the importance of love and understanding.

Another tsunami of emotion welled up inside when she recalled how her own little hand had fit snugly—warm and protected—inside his own, calloused and strong.

"Daddy." The word brought with it a new round of tears, and she slowly dropped to the floor on her knees. "I'm so sorry. I didn't understand. I didn't know what I was doing. I had no idea what you were going through, how you were suffering." She wiped her nose on one sleeve. "I was selfish. I ignored your problems and only focused on mine. I'm sorry, so very sorry. Please forgive me."

The emptying of her regrets forever changed her heart from anger and frustration to understanding and love.

"I love you, Daddy," were the last words she remembered saying before her sobs and shudders finally transitioned into sleep.

Thirty minutes later Sandy awoke with a jolt. Her heart raced as she sat up and looked at her watch. Had it all been a dream?

She slowly stood, brushing the dust off her jeans before walking toward the door. Once there, she turned and scanned the empty warehouse. "He was my dad," she said with firm conviction. "I can do better."

Five minutes later she was busy in the center of the floor with a mop and a bucket.

"I owe him more."

Chapter 22

When Sandy didn't return home for supper, Steve and the girls drove to the old pole barn. The sound of a blaring radio and singing greeted them as they stepped into the freshly cleaned barn. Steve turned toward Emiley and Sarah with his finger pressed against his smiling lips.

For the past few years, and especially the last several months, the love of his life had been angry and depressed. He hadn't seen her dance with abandon since the early years of their marriage, and if she was cranking music and singing inside the barn, he wanted to savor the moment. He also wanted the kids to see their mother genuinely happy.

All three of them shook as they stifled their laughter at the unexpected, and yet delicious, surprise of seeing their wife and mother gyrating in a crazy mop-dance. When Sandy caught sight of them, she motioned them to join her. A few seconds later, Steve and the girls were on the floor embracing their wife and mother.

"Mom! What are you doing?" shouted a laughing Sarah. "Have you lost your mind?"

"Certainly not!" She shouted back, laughing with the same elation with which she danced.

"What's gotten into you, Love?"

Sandy reached over and turned off the radio. "I've been so wrong, Steve. All these years," she admitted. "I've been selfish. I focused on me and ignored the pain in my dad's life. He was a good man. A much better man than I ever realized."

The look of surprise was evident on Steve's face, where a few tears of joy had found their way onto his cheek. He put both hands on his wife's shoulders, kissed her on her forehead, and looked deeply into her eyes. "I can't tell you how happy your change of heart makes me. Makes all of us!"

Sandy nodded. "I know now that during all the important moments of my life, my dad was there for me, Steve."

Emiley cut in. "What do you mean, mom?"

Sandy reached out and pinched her daughter's chin lightly. "Your grandfather was a busy man, honey, but not only did he make time to drive me to Vanguard practices, he patiently taught me to drive. He instilled music in me by giving me my first clarinet, and then my first oboe. I had forgotten so much—or I buried it under my contempt for him. Mom said he cried all the way home after he moved me into my college dorm." She turned back to face her husband. "He cried, Steve. And he was the first one, besides you and me, to hold our children."

She pulled all three closer to her. "My dad loved me unconditionally," she continued, "but until today, until just minutes ago, my contempt for what I thought he'd become clouded my love for him. I lived my entire adult life in unfair judgment of a man who made a lot of mistakes, but a man who loved me despite my many failings and unfair treatment of him."

Steve made a futile attempt to wipe away her happy tears with his fingertips and kissed her softly. Embarrassed as kids tend to be when parents show their affection for one another, Sarah and Emiley took a step back and stared at the floor. But their smiles never left their faces.

"We all can't cry!" Sandy stammered through her laughter. Steve and the girls joined her and together they all shared a long laugh. Sandy sighed. "This was the most important summer of my life. I performed a final service for my dad. I cleaned up a mess that I know he was probably embarrassed to have left. He was simply too frail, too . . . confused . . . to do it himself." She stepped back as if surveying her family. "It was my privilege to do this for him. Someday, somewhere, you may be called upon to perform a final service for someone you love." She paused, placing both hands together on her chest. "It might even be for me. I hope you'll do whatever that may be with a grateful heart. Learn from me and from my mistakes. Let me save you years of pain and frustration. I almost blew it. And if I had, I would have passed this privilege by, not understanding the importance of the opportunity."

"What . . . happened, Sandy?" asked Steve.

"I think a miracle happened," she replied in a softer, more serious tone. "I understand my dad now. My heart has opened to the truth about him. I learned no one did this to me. Rather, I was allowed this sacred opportunity to honor my dad and do for him what he couldn't do for himself. God allowed this to happen so He could do a great work within me. Sam helped me understand all this."

Steve bit his bottom lip as a small furrow crossed his brow. "Go on."

"Sam helped me realize we're all on this earth to serve one another," she continued. "We receive personal blessings so we can be a blessing to others."

Steve exhaled deeply. "So you think Sam brought about this change in you? That God allowed this?"

"Yes. I know it."

"Love, I don't think Sam, or God for that matter, had anything to do with this. They were never really here."

She shook her head, refusing to allow Steve's denial to make her argumentative. "God is here now, and always has been. As for Sam, you saw him, Steve."

"I know you believe all this, but I think you're just tired and overworked." He pulled her close again. "Besides, it really doesn't matter. You've finished the job, you see your dad in an entirely new light. It's all over."

"You're wrong, Steve. It's never over—but that's beside the point," she added. "Weeks ago when you rushed in from court, Sam was here. " She turned and pointed to the north wall a dozen feet to the right of the front door. "Right there. And when you and Tracey came to try to talk to me, he was here in the barn sitting in that same chair."

He stared at the spot his wife indicated before returning his eyes to hers. "I'm sorry. I never saw him. Tracey says she didn't either."

Sandy raised her voice. "I didn't imagine him. He was right there!"

Steve scratched the side of his face, stared back at the spot against the wall and went over to the empty chair. "Sandy . . . Love." He looked at the line in the dust his finger had left weeks before but said nothing as he walked back to his family.

"I can't remember the last time I was this happy. Steve."

With one arm, he pulled her close again. "Come here, Love," and with his other, he brought his girls close in a family hug.

After a few seconds Sandy pulled away. "Come on! Everyone grab a mop and let's finish this together as a family. Emiley, there are two mop buckets over there." With a wave of her right hand, Sandy indicated two empty metal pails against the east wall. "Steve, help her fill them." Turning to her other daughter, she handed a mop to Sarah. "Let's do this for my dad . . . for your grandfather!"

With that, Sandy turned up the radio and together, the Richards family, out of a newfound love and respect for their dad and grandfather, finished cleaning up the superficial debris of his life.

Chapter 23

Sandy's eyes snapped open in her dark bedroom. The clock on the nightstand read 3:16 a.m. She tried to go back to sleep, but thoughts of her father kept her tossing and turning. Finally, at 4:40 a.m., she slipped quietly out of bed, collected the jeans and Vanguard t-shirt she had shed the night before, dressed in the living room, grabbed her keys from the kitchen counter, and headed into the garage.

Thirty minutes later she turned into the driveway leading to the Oakwood National Cemetery. Were the gates locked? She glanced nervously at her watch as second thoughts began creeping into her head. What time did they open? She sighed as she pulled her minivan up, nose to nose with the black wrought iron gate. Desperate times call for desperate measures. She turned off the engine, took a deep gulp of air, opened the door, and stepped outside. She walked slowly along the fence looking for the easiest place to climb. Within a few minutes she was back where she started.

"May I help you?" boomed a male voice from the other side of the gate. A split second later a bright beam of a flashlight exploded in her eyes, temporarily blinding her.

Sandy covered her face with her right hand. "I need to talk to my father."

"Your father?" he replied with more than a bit of skepticism. "It's five-fifteen. The gates don't open until seven."

"Don't you have the key?" she asked.

"Of course I have the key."

"Then what's the problem?"

"The problem is that the cemetery opens at . . ."

"I know," she interrupted. "You told me." She motioned with her hand toward the rows of white headstones standing at attention in long straight rows. "I promise I won't wake anyone."

"Yeah, that's funny lady," shot back the guard. "I could get fired. And that's no joke."

She grinned. "Not unless someone tells. And I would be trespassing. So who would say anything?"

"Mrs. Richards, is that you?" The man's voice changed from authoritative to curious.

"You have me at a disadvantage. I can't see," she replied. "Do I know you?"

"Sure. It's John Craft." The guard turned the flashlight on himself and shined the light under his fleshy chin toward his face. "My son Robbie was your student. His band Arminius is on tour in Europe. You were always his favorite teacher." Lifting a large key from the silver ring attached to his belt, he inserted it into the cemetery lock and the big gate swung open with a metallic groan. "Come in," he whispered. "But hurry and be quiet."

"Thank you, John." Sandy entered quickly and smiled at the man in the security uniform. "This means a lot to me."

"Aww, Mrs. Richards, if it wasn't for you, my son might be a cemetery guard like his old man," replied Craft. "You inspired Robbie to believe in himself, and that he could be and do anything he set his mind to and worked for. That was a great gift to my wife and me."

"How is he? Robbie is very special," she replied. "He's a talented young man who has earned his success through hard work. I'm proud of him. Please tell him hello from me."

"He sure has. A lot a work, I'll tell ya. I can't wait to tell him you asked about him."

"Can I walk down and talk to my dad?" she asked.

"Sure. But let me guide you so you don't trip. It is black as pitch out here."

They found the grave within a few minutes. Once Sandy assured him she was fine, the guard bid her goodbye and left her alone with her thoughts. The rising sun's rays had just begun to reflect off the bright white stones in a luminescent glow. "What a perfect final resting place to honor the men and women who had served our country," she thought.

When she looked down and saw her father's name chiseled on the headstone, Sandy slowly sank to her knees. "Daddy," she whispered, tracing her fingertips along each engraved letter. "It's me... your shadow. I'm sorry I haven't been to see you. I've been busy sorting things out," she began. Oddly, she didn't feel like crying. "I think I've made a mess of my life. I've been angry and judgmental, mostly toward you," she continued. "And in the process, I know I missed out on so much, so many years we should have shared. I think I understand that I made many of the problems you and I had." She smiled, finally feeling the tears beginning to well up inside her. "Okay. You have to admit," she said, smiling through her tears, "you weren't much help, but I should have been more patient, more understanding."

She stopped for a few moments, used her shirt sleeve to dab at her eyes, and soaked in the early dawn's rays. This needed saying. She swallowed hard before continuing. "I've also discovered I'm more like you than I ever thought, Daddy. Since I'm telling you everything, I might as well confess. I'm not going to drink anymore. Last night might have been the first night in years I didn't have at least one glass of wine. I don't know if I'm an alcoholic. Maybe I am. But if not, I'm certain I'm on my way, so I'll stop. I think I can go it alone but if I can't, I'll get help. I promise."

She paused a long while to give her heart time to hear her daddy's reply. A wave of unconditional acceptance swept over her. "I also finished cleaning out your old pole barn, just as I promised," she said, continuing her grave side father-daughter chat. "Thank you for collecting the leaves. I think I may have the world's largest leaf collection." She lowered her eyes until she was looking directly at her daddy's headstone. "I wish you had told me. We could've enjoyed them together. And another thing, I've been talking to a guy named Sam who claims he knew you. It's kind of crazy. I can't imagine how you and he would have known each other. He actually said you were his best friend . . . but I guess it doesn't really matter. The thing is, Sam opened my eyes to so many things, you know? Maybe best of all, he helped me understand that you're not really here. Well, your body is, but you're in a better place, a place that, for a long while, I doubted even existed. It makes me happy and gives me a sense of peace to believe that you hear me. I don't know if you do, but I choose to believe so. If not, I'll repeat it all and more when I see you . . . and for the first time in years, I believe I will see you again. Knowing that fills me with indescribable joy." She wiped at the corners of her eyes as she laughed softly. "Steve says I'm like a new woman. And maybe I am, Daddy. Maybe I am."

Sandy stopped a long while, giving her heart time to catch up to her daddy's reply. Her tears had stopped, and when she continued, her voice was lighthearted and full of joy and contentment. "I'm going to go home now, daddy. I want to make mouse-cakes for your granddaughters. Remember the Mickey Mouse waffle-maker you bought the girls when they were little? I'm going to dig it out today. I pray that idea makes you smile." Raising both her hands, she looked skyward. "Can you believe I just said 'pray'?" She smiled broadly and shook her head. "I'll be back. I promise. Something has changed inside me. I can't explain it, but cleaning your barn somehow cleaned my heart, too. And you know what?" Unexpected tears choked her words and her laughter. "My heart was more cluttered than the barn."

Sandy stood and rubbed away the morning dew from her knees. "I'll be back, and next time I'll bring Steve and the girls." She reached down to touch her father's headstone once more. "I'm so sorry it's been so long since I told you that I love you. Please know that I never stopped loving you . . . I just didn't know it."

Chapter 24

"Get out of bed!" Sandy yelled as she burst into the bedroom.

"What's wrong?" Steve leaped to the floor and stumbled as he grabbed his robe and pulled it on over his cotton pajamas. He followed her into the kitchen where she was already grabbing eggs from the fridge.

"Morning, babe," she said.

Steve stopped in his is tracks. "You haven't called me babe in years," he finally said with a grin as he walked around the kitchen island and spun her around and into his arms. "Who is this happy woman I'm holding captive in my wife's kitchen?" The wonder in his eyes echoed his words.

"I'm still the woman you married," she assured him. "I just left an unhappy imposter in my place for a while."

He leaned back a moment and looked into her eyes. "Really." It wasn't a question as much as a statement of understanding. "And are you going to stick around this time?"

"A stable full of silver unicorns couldn't drag me away from you and our girls," she insisted, kissing her husband softly before pushing him gently away and taking the mixing bowl out of the cabinet. "I'm going to make mouse-cakes."

A roar of laughter poured out of Steve for several seconds. "Mouse-cakes? Do you even know where our old Mickey Mouse waffle maker is?"

The question brought her up short. She closed one eye and thought a moment. "Now, babe, I can't do everything," she teased. "Tell you what, you find it, and I'll make 'em!"

"You don't think the girls might be too old for mouse-cakes?"

"No daddy! We're not!" Emiley and Sarah replied in unison from the hallway. Barefoot and dressed in their pjs and matching smiles, they ran into the kitchen. "Can we help?"

An hour later, Sandy excused the girls and cleared the breakfast dishes with Steve. "I'm going to go change," she announced.

"What's the rush?" asked Steve. "Let's relax today."

"You're coming with me," she continued, "and so is Tracey. We're going to find Sam." She turned to put her arms around Steve's neck. "It's important to me. I don't want anyone thinking I'm crazy."

Steve's arms remained at his side. "Sandy," he began. "It's okay. I love the change I see in you. I have my wife back. I really don't care if this Sam exists or not."

Sandy stiffened. "When you say that, it makes me think you still question my sanity." She reached down and grabbed his hand and pulled him toward the bedroom. "Come on. You need to get dressed too. Tracey is waiting for us."

Twenty minutes later Tracey climbed into the backseat, buckled her seatbelt, tapped Steve's shoulder, and asked. "Have Sandy's meds worn off?"

Steve smiled. "Like the lady says, we're going to find Sam."

Tracey pumped her fist. "I'm going to meet the Walton Center Man of Mystery. Where is he?"

"I don't know," admitted Sandy. "He said he lived around the corner and on the river." She pulled into the pole barn parking lot. "Come on. We'll leave the minivan here and walk."

"Sandy, wait," said Steve as he placed his hand on her shoulder to stop her before she got out. "We don't have to do this. Honestly, this isn't necessary. How about we just let it go?"

Instead of answering, Sandy turned to Tracey. "You're coming, right?"

"Vanguard forever!" replied her friend. "Where you go, I will follow, just like your shadow—Shadow." Tracey firmly slapped the back of Steve's head. "Get it, counselor?"

"Knock it off, Tracey," growled Steve before following after the two women as they walked briskly past the barn.

At the end of the block, Sandy took a left toward the bridge. "Sam said he lived around the corner." She laughed remembering the rest of their conversation.

"What's so funny?" asked Tracey.

"Nothing, really. I asked if he was a troll who lived under the bridge."

"Are you kidding me?" Tracey stopped walking and grabbed Sandy's arm. "Your hot stranger is a homeless guy living under the bridge?"

"This guy is hot?" exclaimed Steve. "I hadn't pictured him as handsome. So what is he, Sandy—an unkempt homeless guy or some hot model-type?" Alarm oozed from Steve's voice.

Sandy dismissed the comment with a flutter of her fingertips. "Oh Steve, that's just Tracey's overactive imagination talking. I think he lives in the apartments across from the bridge. That's about the only place around there."

A few minutes later the trio stopped at the front door of a dilapidated apartment building.

Sandy scanned the faded names on the rusting metal mailboxes stacked one on top of the other outside the front.

Steve looked over her left shoulder. "What's his last name?"

"He never said. All I know is Sam."

Steve leaned closer to the boxes, examined the occupant list, and pushed the black button next to the name Nancy Marvis.

"Who's that?" asked Sandy.

"A client."

A thin woman wearing white short shorts and a tight purple T-shirt answered the door. The wary look on her face vanished when she recognized her attorney. "Mr. Richards? Never thought you'd visit me." The woman leered seductively as she ran her dark brown eyes over Sandy and Tracey. Age lines ran around her mouth and across her hollow cheeks. "Who are they?" she asked with a toss of her bleached blonde shoulder-length hair. Steve knew she was 34, but she looked two decades older. Drugs and hard living did that to people.

"Nancy, this is my wife Sandy and our friend, Tracey."

"Didn't figure you for group fun." Nancy winked before attempting a laugh that ended with several deep coughs. "Come on in!"

Steve offered an uneasy laugh. "No thanks. We're looking for a guy named Sam. Do you know anyone by that name?"

Nancy's eyes narrowed. "Sam who? He a cop?"

"No!" Sandy interjected. "He's a friend, about six feet, a hundred and eighty pounds, light brown hair. Maybe late twenties or early thirties."

Nancy thought a few seconds before shaking her head. "Sorry. No one here comes close to that description."

"Are you sure?" Sandy began. "Sam told me—."

Nancy cut her off mid-sentence. "I'm positive," she smiled, revealing a mouthful of crooked yellow teeth. "This building is full of single moms on welfare, their rug rats, and some old people. If there was a man like you just described, I guarantee you, I'd know him." She winked again, this time at Sandy.

"Thanks, Nancy. Sorry to have bothered you."

"No bother, Mr. Richards. You can stop by anytime. I owe you for keeping me out of jail last time. Hope you find him."

Once the door was closed, Sandy turned to face her husband. "She owes you?"

Steve rolled his eyes. "I got her out of Will County lock-up a few months ago. I'm a lawyer, remember?"

"Soliciting?" Tracey asked.

He shrugged. "You know I can't answer that. Attorney-Client privilege." Steve's gaze returned to the bridge. "What now?"

"Wanna look under the bridge?" Tracey suggested with a sly smile.

"That's an idea, Tracey," shot back Steve, who trotted along the walkway toward the river crossing with Tracey and Sandy keeping up behind him. With the river flowing beneath them, they looked down and spotted two fishermen in a small boat. "Hey!" Steve called as he waved. "Hey, you guys in the boat!"

The fishermen looked up. One of them raised his hand and waved back. "Hey, Steve," he said. "It's me, Izzy Jackson."

"Thinking about jumping?" asked the second man. Both men laughed at the joke.

"Not today," replied Steve. "But I do have a question. "You see anyone camped under the bridge?"

Both men cast a glance under the structure and shook their heads. "Nada," replied Izzy.

"Steve, I can't believe you," huffed Sandy as she turned on her heel and distanced herself from her husband.

"Sandy, wait up!" replied her husband as he chased after her. "He's not in the apartments, where you thought for sure he would be. Honestly, you said he dressed the same way each day. Living in a tent or something under the bridge is not that unrealistic."

"You think I'm crazy!" She turned, hands on her hips.

"Oh, boy. This is going to be good," Tracey muttered under her breath.

"I know you're not crazy," replied Steve softly. "I just thought maybe Sam was a drifter who camped under the bridge. I wasn't making fun of you or questioning your sanity." Steve tried to pull her close, but Sandy pulled back and stood her ground. Steve shot his eyes toward her friend in a plea for help.

"Shadow. Steve's right," offered Tracey. "We're all on the same side, remember? Let's go talk to the police. If Sam's still here, or if he was here and left, they would've seen him. Small town, ya know? You can't be a stranger here long without being noticed, right?" A smile lit up her face. "You never know, maybe the police have him under arrest for soliciting Nancy!"

The last quip triggered a laugh in all three, who turned and headed for the station three blocks away. Tracey linked arms with Sandy and Steve and starting skipping, pulling them along. "Kinda makes you want to sing, 'Hi ho, hi ho, it's off to the pokey we go,' doesn't it?" she asked.

"Do you ever stop?" chuckled Steve with a disbelieving shake of the head.

The eyes of the officer at the front desk widened when the motley trio entered the small station. "Hey, Steve. Mrs. Richards." He nodded toward Tracey. "If she mouths off, teacher or not, I might throw her in the klink for a night," continued the officer while squinting in a fake effort to look mean and serious.

Tracey offered an exaggerated shrug. "Well, then don't pull me over for speeding."

"I won't make that mistake again," he shot back under his breath. He almost sounded serious. The officer settled his attention back on Steve. "What can I do for you today, counselor?"

"Hi, Tom. We're looking for someone," Steve began.

Sandy cut in. "His name is Sam, and we don't know his last name," she explained. She described Sam to the officer, looked at Steve, and then added, "Clean cut and handsome, I guess."

Tracey placed her hand over her mouth, but it did nothing to stifle her laughter. She tapped Sandy on the shoulder and winked. "I don't know if you noticed, but your husband is standing next to you!"

"Sam, huh? Not to my knowledge," replied Tom. "Let me check in the field." Tom picked up the microphone on his desk, clicked a button on the base, and said, "Car Twenty-two. Car Twenty-two."

Tracey laughed a second time. "Good one, Tom! Everyone knows this town only has three police cars!" The officer didn't bother to respond.

"Twenty-two here, dispatch," replied a patrol officer.

"Mike, have you seen a stranger around town recently? Male, six feet or so, one-eighty, brown hair, goes by the name of Sam."

"Don't forget, handsome," Tracey reminded him.

"I'm not going to . . ." began Tom before being interrupted by the responding officer.

"That's a negative, Tom," replied the officer. "I can ask around if you like. What's he done?"

Tom looked up at the trio of faces before him. "When was he here and what's he done?"

"All summer," Sandy replied. "I saw him nearly every day while I was cleaning my dad's old barn." She paused before adding, "And he didn't do anything—criminal, that is. He is just a talker. Certainly not much of a worker."

"You had a stranger helping you clean that old barn?" Tom asked with a sideways glance at Steve. "I'll check with the other two officers, but I've been on patrol most of the summer and haven't noticed any stranger around town. Did he cause any sort of problem?" All three shook their heads. "Then . . . why are you looking for him?"

"We just wanted to thank him, that's all," replied Steve before adding quickly, "It's no problem, Tom. We appreciate your time."

Sandy, Tracey and Steve walked out of the station, back across the bridge, and back toward the old barn without saying a word. When they drew near the building, Tracey asked, "Sandy, how about we see what that old place looks like cleaned out after a long summer of hard work?"

Sandy nodded and unlocked the door.

"Wow!" Tracey said as they walked into the now cavernous-looking structure, the single word bouncing off the exposed walls. "This place is spotless. You did it, girlfriend!"

Together, they all walked into the center of the barn. "I even swept and mopped the floor and knocked down almost all the cobwebs. That alone took hours," announced Sandy before nodding toward one of the corners. "Look—the cobwebs are already coming back, though."

"Got a broom?" asked Tracey? "You missed a spot." She pointed to a small dusty area made all the more conspicuous because of the clean cement around it. "There's a design in it! Cool."

Steve looked down at the dusty spot. His brow furrowed and he turned his head toward his wife. "That's an ichthys."

"A what?" asked Sandy and Tracey in unison.

"An ichthys," he repeated. "A simple fish outline—the symbol Christians used to secretly identify themselves to each other during times of persecution."

"I see them in the parking lot at the school quite often," replied Sandy. "Elijah Sanford's mom has one on her SUV. My kids call it the 'Jesus fish.'"

Tracey scratched the side of her head and swatted at an invisible buzzing insect. "Why'd you draw it?"

Sandy drew a deep breath. "I didn't. Sam drew it with his finger late yesterday afternoon while we were talking. I thought he was just doodling. I could have sworn I mopped the whole place."

"I'll grab that broom," replied Tracey before turning away to find one.

"No!" Sandy grabbed Tracey's arm. "Not yet." Tracey offered a small nod of understanding.

"What's that?" Steve asked, pointing to something metallic and shiny about thirty feet away near the north wall. He walked over, reached down, and picked up a small rectangular piece of metal with rounded edges with a small hole near one end. "Huh," he said. "It's a dog tag. I don't recall seeing it last night, but it was getting dark." He returned to where Sandy and Tracey were standing, turning the tag over in his palm to more closely study it. "I helped clean this floor.

This definitely wasn't here last night. I'm sure of it." Steve looked at his wife. "Was the door locked when got here?"

"Yes. I had to unlock it," replied Sandy.

"It's old," continued Steve as Sandy and Tracey crowded around him. "Maybe World War Two or Korea?"

"There's a lot on there," said Tracey. "Can you read it?"

"Yup. It's all legible," he replied. "William S. Agnello, then a serial number. Looks like the name of his wife or mother—Mildred A. Agnello," he continued. "Then his address. Fifty-one Church Avenue, Brooklyn, New York. Roman Catholic."

Tracey snapped her fingers. "Like my dad," she said. "I have his army dog tags from the war. Two of them on a thin silver chain. It's just like this one."

Steve nodded. "But there's only one here. You have two so that if someone is killed, one is left with the body and the other removed for identification purposes." Steve looked around the rest of the barn floor. "Huh," he said again. "This must have belonged to your dad, Sandy. Maybe it fell out of a box or a bag or something. Here," he added, handing it to his wife. "You should keep it."

"Some have entertained angels unawares."

~ Hebrews 13:2 (KJV)

Epilogue

The phone rang while Sandy was making dinner. She slipped the earring off her left ear and rested the receiver against her shoulder. "Richards' residence."

"Hello, Sandy," said her mother. "Are you free this evening? I need to see to you."

"Actually, I am. Is everything alright?"

"Yes," she replied. "I have something for you."

Dorothy took her daughter's hand and led her down the hallway. "Where are you taking me?" asked Sandy. Without a word her mom turned and entered the small bedroom she had shared with Tom for more than three decades. She and Sandy stood and looked down at a dusty old green trunk.

Sandy frowned. "What's this, Mom?"

Dorothy cleared her throat. When she tried to talk she could not find the words. Several seconds of silence followed. "Your father brought this home from the war," she finally began, her voice little more than a tired old woman's whisper. "It was his army trunk."

Sandy shot her mom a stunned look and studied the box on the floor at the foot of the bed. It looked like a steamer trunk, not quite three feet long, about half as wide, and not quite as deep. It was army green with riveted metal trim and two large leather handles, one on either end. Three hinges lined the front, the two outside latches and a center hatch and lock that required a key to open. Sandy raised her hand to her mouth to softly squeeze her lips when she saw the faded white stenciled letters and numbers running across the top:

```
            SGT. THOMAS S LOUCKS
                 155823—
```

The final numbers of her father's serial numbers looked as though they had been rubbed off or had simply faded into illegibility.

```
        C COMPANY / 1ST BATTALION /
            1ST INFANTRY DIVISION
   Fort Benning - England - Tunisia - Sicily -
      England - Normandy - France - Germany -
             Czechoslovakia - HOME
```

"The boys next door helped me get it down out of the attic," her mother continued. "Your dad left me specific instructions years ago that this was 'for my little girl,' and right before he got sick, he told me you should open it only when you were finished going through the barn."

A shiver worked its way up Sandy's arms and into her body. When her mom pressed a hand against hers, Sandy opened her fingers to hold it. It took a moment to realize her mother was handing her a key.

"What's inside?" asked Sandy softly.

"I don't know honey," she replied. "I never looked, and I never asked. And your dad never told."

Sandy blew out a long breath before inserting the key. The lock was stiff, but a couple jiggles was all it took for the latch to turn. She unclasped the latches and hesitated a moment before lifting the top. It was heavier than she anticipated.

The smell of old cedar wood and a faint trace of moth balls filled the air. The inside of the trunk was lined with a light blue paper stamped with something that looked like a palm tree print—but wasn't. On the back of the top was a small sticker that read "Luggage MFGRS, Wahl Trunk Co., Eau Claire, Wis."

The top portion of the trunk was filled with a wooden insert divided into two equal sections. On the left side was a canvas laundry bag, and on the right a pair of army pants, neatly folded. Sandy lifted the pants. When they unfolded, she spotted a ragged hole high on the right thigh surrounded by what appeared at first blush to be black ink down to the knee. Blood.

She shot her mom a look. "Did you know about this?" the daughter asked of the mother. "About all daddy did during the war?"

Dorothy pursed her lips tightly and nodded. "Of course. I was his wife," she replied, her voice finding its footing now, louder and stronger. "Your dad did more than his share of fighting and killing," she continued. "About ten years ago we were talking late one night and he had more to drink then he should have, and I told him he had gone through hell. He shook his head and said, 'Dotty, I didn't go through hell. I stayed in hell.' I didn't know what to say, so I did what I always did and I just hugged him."

Sandy wiped a small tear away and gently lifted out the wooden divider.

The bottom portion was filled with a ribbon-tied stack of letters addressed from her mom to her dad, some miscellaneous army t-shirts and shorts, all neatly folded, a small but heavy canvas bag with a zipper across the top, and an open envelope with about a dozen photos inside.

Resting on top was a large faded manila envelope with the word "Shadow" written in her dad's hand. She knew because her dad always ended the last line of the "W" with a grand flourish. Sandy slowly sank to the floor and sat cross-legged while her mom sat in a chair next to her.

She carefully opened one end of the large envelope and shook out two smaller ones. The first had her name on it, and even her current address and phone number, all in her dad's hand. The second was addressed to someone whose name she did not recognize. She slowly opened the one addressed to her and began reading:

May 3, 1990

My Dearest Shadow,

Raising you was the greatest gift I ever received, and I know now that God spared me so I could have you.

It is easier for me to write this, sitting here in the middle of the night at the kitchen table, than to tell you. I was never all that good with words—especially after you grew up from a little girl into the beautiful woman, mom and wife that you are.

Please forgive me for not always being there for you in the ways that you needed. I know I am an alcoholic and have other problems. I wish I knew where else to turn for help, but how do you explain to a stranger you want to run through walls, and spend time punching at shadows and shaking your head until you can't see straight to get the thoughts to leave?

I want to give you something to show you how much I love you—and that I didn't forget. How could I forget?

I ask one final favor, too, come to think of it. First, take good care of your mom. I know you will, but it is something I feel better writing. Second, there is a letter here that I wrote long ago to someone. It was returned to me unopened. I tried hard for many years but I could not find the recipient. You can read it. In fact, you should read it. But my last wish is that you find a way to track down the family and get the letter to them.

I love you with all my heart.

Daddy

By this time Sandy was sobbing so deeply she could barely breathe. She handed the letter to her mother to read. Soon, both women were crying.

A few minutes later, once she blew her nose and had a glass of water, Sandy was back at the foot of the bed staring at the second envelope. It was addressed to a Mrs. William S. Agnello, 51 Church Avenue, Brooklyn, New York. The three-cent stamp in the upper right corner was cancelled, and across the envelope at an angle was stamped the words "Addressee Not Known. Return to Sender." The envelope was still sealed.

Dorothy leaned over and handed Sandy a letter opener. "Use this so you don't damage it."

Sandy slid the silver tip into the envelope and slid it slowly along the edge. As she unfolded two sheets of thin, ivory-colored paper, a thick lock of brown hair fell out. She caught the tuft in her left hand, looked at it for a brief moment, and closed her fingers around it. This letter was typed. Trembling, she began reading aloud:

July 2, 1944, France

Dear Mrs. Agnello,

    My name is Thomas Loucks. I am a sergeant in the same company as your husband, Corporal Agnello. I waited a while until I was assured you had by this time received news of the death of your husband. I was also busy during much of this period fighting the krauts.
    I didn't know Agno before I entered the Army, but we became fast and dear friends. I wanted to share these thoughts with you because he told me many times if something happened to him, to write to you because any info I could provide would give you comfort. It would pain me to know I did not perform my duty for my friend, so here is my promise fulfilled. I hope it helps you as he hoped it would.
    I remember the moment we met. It was like we had known each other for years even though opposite in most ways. He was a big city boy from New York, and I am from a tiny little place over 300 miles south of Chicago called Sesser, Ill. That never mattered to us. I know I'll never have another friend like Agno again, nor will I ever forget him.

Sandy stopped and shot a quizzical look at her mom. "Agno. I know that name." Unable to place it, she continued reading:

Your husband and I were part of the first wave to hit Omaha Beach. I know his death must grieve you so, but Agno was killed instantly and almost immediately. I was holding him when he died. He did not suffer.
    After we secured the beachhead, a shell nearly knocked me out and I did not advance with my company for about 24 hours. The next morning, men from Graves Registration arrived to organize the bodies for temporary burial. They asked for volunteers. When we went back to where Agno was, I told a major that he was my friend and am not ashamed that I broke down. The

major, a deeply religious man, told me, "This is the final service you can perform for your friend. Through this Hell, amidst all this killing and dying, I have come to know that God has placed us on this earth to be servants to each other."

    He called up a litter and together we carried your husband to a shallow trench and buried him there shoulder to shoulder with other brave men. I used my handkerchief to clean his face, cut a lock of hair from his head, and put a thin blanket over his body. I removed one of his dog tags and put it on a stake. Rest assured he will be identified and moved to a proper cemetery soon. We removed his dog tags so he could be properly identified.

Sandy gasped. Agno was the name the therapist had mentioned in her office. When she told this to her mother, Dorothy nodded her understanding. Sandy turned her eyes back to the letter:

    I'm not much of a religious man, but I prayed to God that the work I had done was pleasing to Him and to Agno. I thanked God for the brief but powerful wartime friendship your husband and I shared. If it weren't for this awful war, this would be a beautiful place to visit. If they keep him buried here, I hope it is high on the bluff overlooking the beaches.

Sincerely,

Sgt. Tom "Duke" Loucks
U.S. Army

Sandy's hands shook as she set the letter down. There was so much she wanted to say, but she was unable to say anything at all. Her mother stood and rubbed her daughter's shoulder. "I am going to make some tea," she finally said. "I'll bring some back while you go through the rest of the things."

Sandy nodded, reached into the trunk, and gently shook the envelope of photographs until they spilled out. Most were of her father as a young soldier. The first was in his dress uniform. She turned it over and looked at the back for more information. In another, he was standing with a rifle in his hand, and a third posed with a massive sand dune behind him. Several more featured the handsome sergeant with a handful of his buddies. All young. All smiling. All still alive. She turned the last one over, but the back was blank, just like all the others.

Her legs cramping, Sandy stood and stretched, her mind awash with a hundred thoughts and feelings that triggered a blur of emotions. It was then her eye caught sight of the corner of something sticking out from between the folds of the canvas laundry bag in the wooden partition. She eased back the edge to discover a brass picture frame holding an oversized black and white image. The black felt backing had come unglued, so when she picked up the frame the photo slipped out and fell facedown onto the bag. Unlike the smaller unframed images, there was something written in pencil on the back of this one:

May 28, 1944, England
Me and Cpl. William Samuel Agnello

Sandy turned the photo over and looked at the front. Her dad was on the left, smiling broadly with his arm around the shoulder of another man who was wearing an off-white T-shirt and khaki pants tucked into shiny black boots.

A few second later, from out in the kitchen, Dorothy heard a loud scream from the bedroom. After a second of silence came another scream, louder than the first.

In the bedroom, a thick tuft of light brown hair fell out of a shaking hand and fluttered softly onto the carpet.

The phone rang three times before a woman's voice answered. "Hello?"

"Is this Mrs. Ardovino?" asked Sandy. "You live in Chicago?"

"Yes, but please call me Rose. Who's this?"

Sandy took a deep breath and continued. "I'm sorry to bother you, Mrs. Ardo—Rose," she began. "My father served in the Second World War and I just found his Army trunk. It had some information inside, including some photos, and I think you might be related to one of his Army friends."

"Oh? Well, that's interesting. How may I help you?" she asked.

"I am trying to learn more about my dad," Sandy explained. "I was wondering if you could answer a few questions."

"I'll try," replied Rose. "But I don't really know much about the war."

"Are you related to William Samuel Agnello?"

"Yes—Sam Agnello was my father," Rose slowly replied. "I never knew him because he was killed in the war. I was just two when he died."

"Your mother, did she live on Church Avenue in Brooklyn during the war?"

Several seconds of silence followed before she answered. "I was born there," began Rose. "My mom moved us back in with her parents in the summer of 1944 right after my dad was killed." She paused before asking, "How do you know all this? And why are you asking me these questions?"

"That explains why the letter was returned," Sandy whispered.

"What letter?" asked Rose. "What are you talking about?"

"Rose," began Sandy, "I just have one more question to ask you. And then I promise I will explain everything. It's very important—for both of us."

"Okay," replied an obviously hesitant voice on the other end of the line.

"Your mother. Did she die of cancer?"

Rose let out a small gasp. "Yes. Just two years ago. She never got over my father's death, and she never remarried."

Sandy ran her hand across the top of her dad's Army trunk. "I think we are going to be good friends, Rose. And we have a lot to talk about. I don't even know how to begin. Can I buy you a cup of coffee?"

Afterword

Post-traumatic stress disorder, or PTSD, can affect generations of families, as Gary W. Moore's *The Final Service* makes abundantly clear.

Sandy's mother Dorothy, for example, had no idea what to do to help her husband. Like many spouses then and now, she avoided the issue and the stigma associated with what, during World War II, was often called "shell-shock." Dorothy handled what she did not fully understand by simply sweeping it under the rug and looking the other way. Her decision, and Tom's invisible wounds, went on to engulf Sandy, and in turn, her own family and Tom's and Dorothy's grandchildren.

As Moore's story highlights, diagnosing "shell-shock," or what would come to be known as PTSD, is and was very difficult. As it unfolds, piece by piece, *The Final Service* does an excellent job unraveling Tom's quiet suffering and connecting his experiences to PTSD and its related issues to the problems between father and daughter.

Sandy's emotional journey and the revelations that come to light are as realistic as they are uplifting. Because Moore's characterization of the story's protagonist is often gloomy and disheartening, her progression into lightness and healing is refreshing. He portrays the long and difficult journey for compassion and understanding that ultimately frees Sandy from the generational turmoil in a believable way. *The Final Service* is filled with characters that are all too familiar to me, for I deal with them on a daily basis—their stories, their suffering, their anxieties, their heartaches.

Today, the medical profession has a much clearer understanding of post-traumatic stress disorder and the many ways in which to treat it. It is indeed a very real ailment with tangible and too often heart-wrenching consequences that not only include alcoholism and depression, but drug abuse, physical and mental abuse, divorce, and even suicide.

Moore's story also sheds light on the importance of having a strong support system in order to both alleviate the stress and fight this terrible (though now much better understood) consequence of war. Because of this, readers will better understand the extreme dynamics of depression, alcoholism, and other characteristics of PTSD in their veteran family members and friends. Hopefully, it will also convince everyone to reach out to veterans in any way they can, if only to show appreciation for their service.

It is important that we all join together to assist veterans and their family members as they continue their own physical and psychological battles here at home. Today's veterans and their families deserve to know that they are supported just as much at home as they are and were abroad.

If you know or suspect someone is suffering from PTSD, it is important to seek help from a medical professional. I suggest contacting your local mental health care professional. Your family doctor can help you find the right assistance and trained professional to guide the veteran and his loved ones through this traumatic time.

My work in this area, which includes educating people across the country about PTSD, together with other information, can be found at www.TheBattleContinues.org.

— Sudip Bose, MD, FACEP, FAAEM

Dr. Sudip Bose is an Iraq war veteran, recognized as a "CNN Hero" for receiving the Bronze Star and serving as the U.S. physician who treated Saddam Hussein after his capture. Dr. Bose is widely recognized as one of the "Leading Physicians of the World" by the International Association of Healthcare Professionals and one of the world's leading experts on PTSD. He is the founder of www.TheBattleContinues.org, a nonprofit charity.

The Des Plaines / Skokie Vanguard
"Go Big Red!"

"If you were in The Vanguard, no explanation is needed.
If not, no explanation is possible."

— Sandy Richards

Two members of the rifle squad of color guard of the 1973 Des Plaines Vanguard Drum & Bugle Corps. *Jane Boulen*

Drum & Bugle Corps is a unique American art form that is both music and sport. The Des Plaines Vanguard was an inaugural member of Drum Corps International (DCI) and world class leader in innovation and execution. They passed into history after the 1976 competitive season, but their influences and impact can still be seen in today's marching music.

For those of us who knew and loved the Des Plaines Vanguard, the corps lives on in our hearts and minds. But for those who have never heard of this incredible organization, or are unfamiliar with drum & bugle corps, I hope Sandy and her story influence you to learn more about it at www.desplainesvanguard.com, or about Drum Corps International at www.dci.org.

Acknowledgments

Writing this story while looking at life through another person's eyes has been an especially revealing experience. Let me begin these acknowledgments by thanking "Sandy," the inspiration for this story whose name has been changed to preserve her anonymity. I still vividly recall the day she shared her true-life struggle with me, and how it planted the seeds of this story. Thank you, Sandy. I hope you approve.

I want to thank my agent Tris Coburn of Tristram C. Coburn Literary Management for his efforts and encouragement. My stories don't fit into a single category or genre publishers generally seek. My tastes tend to be eclectic and the idea of writing over and over on a similar subject or an ongoing series with the same hero holds little interest for me. I like to write what interests me, and my tastes and interests are all over the chart. Tris continues to find a home for my writing and the book you hold in your hand is proof of his success.

I also want to thank my friend and publisher Theodore P. Savas at Savas Beatie for recognizing the light in this story and how it may not only entertain, but help create understanding and awareness. Ted is a dedicated supporter of the men and women who serve in the armed forces of our country and appreciated the need to share this story with a wide audience. This is our third book together. My adventures with Savas Beatie began with *Playing with the Enemy* and continued with *Hey Buddy* and now *The Final Service*. Thank you, Ted, marketing director Sarah Keeney, and the entire team. I hope we can make it four!

At Ted's suggestion, Tim Hartman joined us by agreeing to draw the Loucks' barn, which appears as book's frontis piece. Tim has been professionally acting, singing, writing, cartooning and storytelling in Pittsburgh, Pennsylvania, since 1982. Though known primarily for his work on the stage (including two appearances on Broadway), Tim is also an award-winning political cartoonist and storyteller. You can see more about Tim here: www.timhartman.com.

Thank you to my dear friend Bonnie Latino. Bonnie is a married to a wonderful man and veteran, Colonel Tom Latino. Tom and Bonnie are American patriots and supporters of our men and women in uniform. Bonnie, the author of the outstanding book *Your Gift to Me* (2014), has been both my editor and muse, but mostly a friend. She has a knack for telling me that I'm pretty good at this craft, especially when I feel like God skipped past me when he was passing out writing talent. Perhaps Bonnie is my Sam.

Thank you to my children Toby, Tara Beth, and Travis, and my son-in-law Jeff Leach. They are our living legacy and proof that we were here. If they are any reflection of this coming generation, we're in great shape. Thank you. I love you all.

Now I get to rave about my grandsons! Thank you to the two incredible young men to whom this book is dedicated, Caleb Daniel Leach and Noah Moore Leach. The joy you bring to my life is indescribable. Never forget how much your Nana and Papa love you. Your Nana and Papa begin every morning praying for your happiness, health, safety and prosperity. Our greatest prayer is that grow up to be men of God, loving Him and loving others.

There are no adequate words of thanks and praise for the love of my life. Arlene Wigant Moore is a woman of great strength and deep faith. As I type this, we are approaching our fortieth wedding anniversary. For this reason alone, I consider myself the luckiest man on earth. Thank you, Arlene, for hanging with me for all these years. I promise you, our best years together are in our future and not in our past.

Above are a partial list of my friends and family. They are blessings in my life, so I am compelled to thank my Lord and Savior Jesus Christ, from whom all blessings flow. Thank you for my friends, family, career and opportunities. I pray that I reflect You through all that I do.

The Final Service
(the movie)

Produced by Positivity Pictures, LLC
(in conjunction with CinemaFund Capital Management, LLC)

In pre-production now!

Directed by academy award-winner Kieth W. Merrill,
who has also written the screenplay.

Toby Moore ("A Separate Peace," "First Daughter,"
"Murder in Greenwich," "Law & Order," "C.S.I. Miami") has been
signed to play "Sam," with the balance of the cast and
a shooting schedule to be announced soon.

See www.thefinalservice.com for more details!

Karen Kring

About the Author

Gary W. Moore is known worldwide as an inspirational and motivational speaker, successful entrepreneur and businessman, accomplished musician, and author.

He penned the award-winning *Playing with the Enemy: A Baseball Prodigy, World War II, and the Long Journey Home* (Savas Beatie, 2006; Penguin, 2008), the story of his father Gene Moore and his remarkable life in baseball and war, and the acclaimed *Hey Buddy: In Pursuit of Buddy Holly, My New Buddy John and My Lost Decade of Music* (Savas Beatie, 2011). He was also a contributing author to the best-selling Chicken Soup for the Soul series.

In addition to his writing, Gary has been a mainstay in the business world for decades. He was the CEO of several public and private companies, and is currently Co-CEO of the Moore Alliance and a partner in CinemaFund Capital Management, LLC, and Positivity Pictures, LLC.

Gary and his wife Arlene have been married for more than four decades and reside in Bourbonnais, IL.